CHAS WILLIAMSON
Paradise Series: Book Three

COURAGE
in Paradise

Print ISBN: 978-1-64649-053-0

eBook ISBN: 978-1-64649-054-7

 Year of the Book
135 Glen Avenue
Glen Rock, PA 17327

Dedication

Courage in Paradise is a special book to me. It deals with having the courage to do what's right, even when every indicator is telling you to do something else. I learned all I need to know about courage from the woman this book is dedicated to—my wife, my sweetheart, my soulmate. You, my love, have been the absolute best influence on me since the day we met. You've been my teacher, not just telling me, but showing me how to act in the face of adversity. You've taught me about love, how to love and how to be loved. You are my greatest fan, encouraging me to not only dream, but to chase those dreams and make them real, even when the world is full of doubt. I am who I am because of you. I hope you are proud of the man you've helped me become because I'm so very proud of you, and me, and wonderfully proud of us. No honor I'll ever have, no title or achievement, could ever mean as much as having your love. And because of that, at the end of my life, I can honestly say, *we lived happily ever after.*

Acknowledgments

To God, for delivering the heaping blessings you've given to me.

To my best friend, for being everything to me.

To Demi, for your guidance along the way.

To my beta readers, Connie, Mary, Sarah and Janet, for your suggestions, help and tweaks to make my words better.

To artists and influences such as Taylor Swift, Luke Bryan, Brad Paisley, Patti Loveless, Patsy Cline and others, who inspire by your words and music (and provide the soundtrack in my mind).

To my children and grandchildren. These silly romance stories I write are my legacy to you, and when I'm gone, when you read these stories, know they were written with you in mind. No man in history has been as blessed as I am.

For teachers and authors who've inspired me by opening my mind to worlds I would have never known or imagined and for helping me use the creativity God placed in my heart and soul. My prayer is that my words will someday touch others as you have influenced me.

Prelude

E mma opened the microwave door and removed the steaming bowl of venison stew. Tonight was one of the rare occasions when she had to eat alone. Her brother Mikey had left earlier for hockey practice and her parents were off, celebrating their anniversary. The house shuddered from the cold Canadian winter wind. *After dinner, I'll read by the fire until Mikey gets home.*

As she took her first bite, noise from outside caught her attention. It sounded like car tires on crusted snow, but she hadn't seen any lights. *Who could it be?* Emma walked to the door and looked out the window, straining her eyes against the darkness. Yes, there was a car idling near the barn, exhaust curling around the fenders. Emma didn't recognize it. She flipped the switch to turn on the yard light. The sight made her mouth dry. Four men were hurrying through the snow toward the house. Even from a distance, Emma could see masks over their faces. One was carrying what looked like a crowbar.

*Dear Lord, help me! W*hat had Mom told her if there was an emergency? *Make sure the door's* *locked and turn off the lights.* Emma did and then reached into her pocket for her cell. She quickly speed-dialed Mikey's phone. Almost immediately, she heard his ringtone. Emma whipped around and spotted his device on the edge of the table. *I need help and you forgot your phone!*

Emma ran upstairs to her bedroom, turned off the lights and stuffed herself into the farthest corner of the closet. She covered up with some blankets from the floor. Her next action was to call the Royal Mounted Police. The telephone was answered almost immediately.

"Please help! I'm home alone and there are four masked men outside. I'm scared."

"Give me your name and address."

Emma's reply was interrupted by noises echoing from the kitchen... and the sound of breaking glass.

The dispatcher's voice was firm, but calm. "Help's on the way. Don't hang up. Put the phone on speaker and keep the line open. I'll stay on here with you. Be as quiet as you can."

A deep voice resonated through the house. "You two find that girl while we search for other valuables."

Emma struggled not to cry as she heard the sounds of banging and crashing. *They're trashing the house.* She held her breath when her room light filtered under the closed door. The light intensified and she realized she was exposed. Suddenly a hand grabbed her foot.

"Hey. Lookie what I found!"

Emma struggled, but he was too strong. The man pulled her from the closet. "No!" she cried. "Please don't hurt me!"

The masked intruder laughed as he yanked her by the arm and tossed her across the room. He then shoved her onto the bed and pointed a finger at her face. "Don't move and I won't hurt you."

A second man entered the room. "You Emma Campeau?"

"Y-yes. What do you want?"

Through his mask, he questioned her. "Anyone else here?"

Emma managed a whimper. "No."

The second man grabbed her chin and squeezed her face so they were eye to eye. "Lie to me, girl, and I'll make you sorry you were ever born. Now tell me the truth. Anybody else here?"

"No, no. Please don't hurt me. I'm being honest."

"Where'd the big man go? We watched him drive off."

"He-he went to hockey practice."

"When will he be back?"

"I dunno. Maybe nine or ten."

The first one laughed. "More than enough time to have a little party. This one's pretty, and young."

The second man turned and punched the first masked man so hard it drove him to the floor. "Like I told you and your brother, she is *not* to be touched." He ground his boot against the other man's hand. "Understand me?"

"Yeah, yeah. I forgot. Sorry."

The second man turned to Emma. "As you can see, I'm a man you don't want to mess with. Now answer me. Any valuables in the house?"

"Just mom's jewelry. We don't have much."

The first man struggled to his feet. The mask across his mouth did little to filter out his bad breath. "There any money?"

Emma's eyes were blurry and she became sick to her stomach. "M-my wallet's in my purse. Over on the chair. Take it and, and, and leave. Please?"

Two other men entered the room. One carried a steel bar. "Ain't much here. I grabbed the silverware and some necklaces. Thought you said they had cash."

The man with bad breath grabbed her purse and emptied it on the bed. He rummaged through the contents. "Fifteen dollars? That's it? You holding out on us?"

"N-no. We don't keep a lot around the house. Please, take it and, and go. I w-won't tell anyone."

He threw her purse away, grabbed her arm and pulled Emma toward him. "Not even worth breaking in here. What do we do with her?"

The man who was obviously in charge uttered something Emma couldn't quite hear. Then the one behind let go of her arm. "Grab a coat, girl. You're coming with us."

Emma stood and tried to back into the corner. "No, I don't want to go!"

"I don't believe I asked. That was an order. Get your coat on." He took a menacing step toward her. "Don't make me have to repeat myself..."

Before the man could finish, a voice called out from downstairs. "Emma? Came back to get my phone." Then the voice changed. There was an urgency in it now. "What da hell? Emma. Where be you? Emma?"

Emma screamed. "Run!" A hand slapped her, the force knocking her to the floor on the other side of the bed. Emma struggled to turn and see what was happening.

The door flew open and her brother filled the door frame. Rage covered his face, but before he could speak, the man with the iron bar swung it, hitting her brother in the face. Mikey held a hand across his bloody mouth and spit two teeth to the floor. Her brother's face was as red as the blood on his hand. The man with the crowbar hauled back and went to strike again, but Mikey was quicker. His massive left hand caught the crook of the tool and his right easily stripped the weapon from the brute. Mikey grasped the bar as a club and knocked his attacker to the floor. Quickly he moved between Emma and the invaders. "Git in the corner or I'll use dis." He shook the crowbar at the men. "Stand behind me, Emma."

Emma ran behind Mikey's massive body and peeked around at the intruders. "I called the Mounties. They're on their way."

Mikey handed his keys to Emma. "Good job, sis. Go sit in my truck. Anyone but me leaves dis house, you hightail it for town."

Emma was confused. "What?"

Her brother nodded. "Remember what Daddy always says? The strong, dey take care of da weak. You be leavin' now."

"I won't leave you."

Her brother laughed and the tone sent shivers up her spine. "Dis is a learnin' moment and it's my turn to be da teacher, sis. No need for you to see dis. Go wait in the truck."

"But Mikey..."

He stepped backwards, forcing her into the hall. "It be fine. Remember, anyone but me steps outside, you git."

The big man entered her room and closed the door quietly behind him. His voice roared from inside. "Boys, we ain't properly been introduced. Name's Mickey Campeau and I'm gonna teach you never to prey on da weak again, eh?"

Chapter 1

R iley Espenshade removed breakfast from the microwave, dropping the steaming sandwiches on paper plates. She grabbed two bottles of water from the refrigerator. "Here you go, kid. Eat up. Sam said they'd get here around eight with the truck."

The beautiful young blonde standing across the bar took the food and smiled at Riley. "You're so kind. Getting me that interview and then inviting me to share an apartment with you. I really liked the Lancaster area when you drove me around. And your family... Don't know how to say thank you."

Riley laughed. "That's what friends do for each other in my neck of the woods. I never planned on staying in Cleveland to begin with. It's been fun, but I'm ready to go home."

Didi Phillips grinned at her. "I'm so glad to be moving with you to... what's the town again?"

"Lititz. We're moving to Lititz. Just far enough from Harrisburg to make it enjoyable."

They ate quietly until Didi broke the silence. "So, have you heard from your hockey player lately? Has he asked you out yet?"

Riley's chest warmed at the thought of Mickey Campeau. Just like he promised, he'd called her the night of Harry and Ashley Campbell's wedding. "Not yet. He spent the summer with his sister in Knoxville, then went on vacation. But he's called me every couple of days."

Didi laughed. "Oh, yeah? What about seeing him?"

Riley sighed. "He said maybe when he gets back to Philly. Look, I'm not putting a lot of faith in this man. He's a pro sports star and has a bad-boy reputation."

Didi wiped her mouth with a paper towel. "You're still upset about Teddy, the baseball pitcher. The one you dated."

Riley nodded. "Yep. I was really into him. But he wanted more than I was willing to give and when I said 'no', he dropped me like a sack of trash and moved on to the next girl in line."

Didi walked around the bar and hugged Riley. "You did the right thing, but maybe Mickey's different. Not all men are the same."

Riley shook her head and laughed. "And you're speaking from experience? I don't think you've been on a date since I've known you."

Didi's face turned pink and she looked away. "I just haven't met the right man." Then she mumbled something under her breath.

Riley thought she knew what her friend was thinking. She *had* met a man—Riley's brother Sam. He'd spent almost three months living with Riley after Kyle Parker broke his leg. Didi developed a massive crush on Sam and things were about to get out of hand on Christmas Eve, but Riley arrived home in time to put a stop to it. Her brother finally came to his senses and returned east. To the woman who was waiting for him. The one who was now his wife, Hannah. "Give it time, young lady."

Before Didi could respond, a knock came at the door. Didi rushed to open it. The young man standing with a cane smiled at her friend. Didi engulfed him with a hug. "Sam. So great to see you."

"Nice to see you, too." He unraveled himself from the girl and hobbled over to embrace his sister. Sam gave Riley a peck on the cheek. "Sis, I missed you. Time to take you home."

"I'm ready. How's Hannah, and my nieces?"

Sam shot her that crooked smile she loved. "Fine. Hope you don't have plans tonight. My wifey-poo's making dinner and she baked a special cake to celebrate. The whole family will be there." He turned to Didi. "Hannah said you should come, too."

Didi frowned. "Thanks, but it sounds like a family thing."

Sam nodded. "It is. You're family now. Hannah will have my hide if you don't come."

Riley stared at her brother. *That's strange.* At Sam's wedding, Hannah sensed Didi had a crush on Sam and had ferociously questioned Riley about it. Of course, Riley hadn't told her new sister-in-law about Sam and Didi almost kissing.

Another man's voice echoed from the hall. "Okay. We're burning daylight. I *do* want to spend *some* time with Ashley tonight. We're newlyweds, you know?" It was Harry Campbell, Sam's best man and apparently, new best friend. *Hmm.* Riley knew her brother once had a crush on Harry's wife, Ashley, when they were kids. Sam had confided she was the first girl he ever kissed. But now, the two couples seemed to hang around together all the time.

Didi stuck out her hand. "Hi, Harry. This was nice of you to help us move."

Harry shook it briefly and nodded. "Didi."

Didi giggled and nodded in return. "Harry."

Riley wiped the crumbs from her hands. "Okay. Let's start. You and I can carry out the big stuff, Harry."

A third man's deep voice caught her attention. "Nope. You supervise, eh? Picking up da heavy stuff. That's why I be here." Riley turned to stare at the man who stood at the door. Mickey Campeau.

Chapter 2

M ick slid the last drawer into the dresser. He turned to see Riley staring at him with a happy smile on her face. Riding all the way back from Ohio with her was incredible, the best day of his life. A lightheartedness filled his chest. "Looks like we be done, no?"

Riley laughed at him and nodded, her pretty face making him tingle. His mind traced back to the first time he'd seen it. Mick had been so tired of the type of women who were attracted to him, the ones his sister Emma called 'gold diggers'. Mick had been searching the web, typing in 'drop dead gorgeous women'. Riley had been on the fifth page, but something about her smile touched him. When he clicked on the photo, he read she was a sportscaster for a Cleveland television station. He'd tuned in to watch her sportscast the next morning and was hooked.

"Anyone ever tell you that you talk funny?"

He chuckled and winked. "Better than lookin' funny, eh?"

Her smile left. "Thank you. It was such a surprise when you showed up this morning."

Mick stretched, his back muscles tight from the six-hour drive from Ohio. "Ya' think? It was a bigger one for me when I ran into ya at da wedding." He felt his smile leave as he took her in. "Seems like fate had us planned ta meet. Never dreamed when I stopped along the street to help poor Ashley, when dem guys were pickin' on her, dat I'd finally meet you."

Riley's eyes grew large. "Explain to me again how you already knew who I was."

He roared with laughter. "That be easy. Saw your picture one day on the internet. Was surfin' along and den, der you were. Maybe it was the Big Guy who did it."

Riley blushed and straightened her shirt. The girl looked away from him. She was even more beautiful today than he remembered. Even without makeup. And his memory of her from the wedding was hard to top. Mick had never met anyone prettier.

Her brother Sam hobbled into the room. "You guys ready to head to our place?"

Mick eyed him strangely. "For what?"

Sam smacked his head. "Sorry. Forgot to invite you. Dinner's at our house. You are coming, aren't you?" Sam glanced at his sister and smiled deviously. "That is, if Riley *wants* you to come."

Her face was beet red when she turned to Mick and nodded. "Yes, please."

He sighed. Mick was hoping to take her someplace romantic for the first date. "Maybe not. I should be headin' back. Been a long day, ya know? Harry got me up at one-thirty this morning ta drive out there. I still got two more hours back home."

Riley frowned, the color in her face draining away. "I guess, if you really want to leave."

Harry's voice boomed behind them. "Nonsense. You're staying at our place. Ashley would insist."

Riley reached for Mick's hand. The warmth of her fingertips sent wonderful sensations up his arm. "Please? I'd like you to meet my parents."

Mick swallowed hard. *Meet her folks? Dis be real?* "I guess I could, but only on one condition."

Riley's eyes curled at the corners when she smiled. "And that is?"

"We do breakfast tomorrow, us alone. My treat, eh?"

Her entire face broke out in a grin. "I'd be honored."

Mick rode shotgun with the little blonde girl in the back. She was nice and pretty, but didn't compare to Riley.

Didi spoke up. "Sam said the entire family. Who all will be there?"

Riley stopped at an intersection and looked both ways before continuing toward Strasburg. "My parents and the four foster kids. I believe Harry and Ashley will also be there. Of course, Sam and his wife, Hannah, and their daughters. He has two, Mick—Beth and Missi."

"I remember dem. Da little one's cute. The girl widout her front teeth, eh?"

Riley laughed. "Um-hmm. Tell Didi what you did at the wedding."

Mick removed his dental plate and turned to the blonde, minus his two front teeth. "I smiled and she asked if da Tooth Fairy paid me." He turned away, reinserted his teeth and pivoted back toward the younger girl. "Said no. Carry mine wid me, all da time."

Didi recoiled. "That's gross."

Both Mick and Riley roared with laughter, then shouted out loud together, "That's what she said."

Didi shook her head. "You two. It's like you're made for each other."

Mick turned and looked out the window. His face was warm. *I sure be hopin' so.*

***

It looked like it might rain. As Riley pulled in, she caught sight of Harry, Sam and her father raising easy-up canopies to cover the patio tables. Sam and Hannah had such a beautiful place. *And their love's turned it into a home.* Riley and Mick walked onto the porch with Didi a couple of steps behind them.

The door flew open and Hannah, Sam's wife, poured through. She hugged Riley and kissed her cheek. "So glad to see you."

Riley's heart swelled. While Hannah would never replace her dead sister, Jenna, there was such a closeness between them. "I'm happy to see you, too. Now that I'm back in Lancaster, I'm sure we'll see each other all the time."

"Ahem." It was Mick. *Almost forgot about him.*

"Hannah, you remember Mickey from Ash's wedding?"

Riley forced back a giggle when she caught the look on her sister-in-law's face. Hannah was starstruck. Mick bowed. "Nice to see ya' again, ma'am." He turned to Riley. "Think I'll give da men a hand with dem tents, if'n you don't mind."

"Sure. I'll be out shortly."

The three women watched him walk away. Despite his size, he was quite agile. Didi's soft whistle broke the silence. "Riley, you didn't tell me how hot he is. You could have warned me."

Her face heated. Hannah picked up the line of teasing. "Yeah, Riley's been keeping him under wraps, like a pirate with buried treasure."

Out of the corner of her eye, Riley caught the wink Hannah shot Didi. "Maybe you were right, Didi. You might have to crash over here tonight, you know?" The two women burst out in laughter.

Riley whipped around to face her young friend. "You know me better than that." She turned to Hannah. "And you do, too. Who supported you when my brother was acting like an idiot? I'm pretty sure you owe me, big time."

Hannah hugged her again. "I certainly do, but it's so much fun to tease you. Hey, just wondering— how are you going to introduce him to Mom and Dad?"

"What do you mean?"

"I mean, will you tell them he's just a friend?"

Didi interrupted, "How about saying he's your boyfriend?" The little blonde's lips were curled into a smile. "You realize, Hannah, he's called her almost every day since the wedding and..."

Riley pointed a finger in Didi's face. "Keep in mind, those who live in glass houses shouldn't throw stones. I know a secret or two about you..." *Keep it up and I'll let Hannah know you once made out with Sam.*

Didi's face turned pink, seemingly reading Riley's mind. "Sorry. I was just kidding."

Hannah's smile didn't leave. "Wow. This is great intel. Didi, maybe you *should* stay here tonight... I could use more information about this romance."

Riley's mouth dropped open as she turned to Hannah. "*Et tu*, Brute?"

Hannah winked. "Better decide what you're going to say soon. It's time to eat." Her brother's wife motioned to Didi. "Can you give me a hand carrying out the food? Riley, would you mind setting the tables? Sam took the plates and silverware out earlier."

"Uh, sure." Riley turned and headed toward the patio. A serious debate was going on between her heart and her mind. *How* should *I introduce him? Do I think of him as a friend or... more?* Her heart softly answered. *You know what you really want to say.*

Chapter 3

The station manager met them at the conference room door. "Well ladies, orientation's over. I'd like to introduce you to the film crews you'll be working with." Didi's eyes gravitated to the middle-aged woman and the young man standing behind her. "This is Monica Mitchneck. She'll be your camera woman, Riley. Didi, this is Luke Zinn. He's your camera guy."

Didi briefly glanced at Luke. Nothing special, especially with the two-day beard, Luke Bryan shirt and uncombed hair. She smoothed the solid black dress she wore, before offering her hand. "Hi, I'm Deidre Phillips, but please call me Didi."

His hand was warm in hers. "Seen your photo, but it didn't do you justice. The camera will love you." Didi's face warmed when she saw the twinkle in his eye.

Beside her, Monica and Riley were getting acquainted. Riley turned to the manager. "So what are we doing for the rest of the day?"

The lady smiled. "Publicity videos. You and Monica will head to some of the local stadiums for background shots." She turned to Didi. "And you two travel to some of the local hotspots for your film. Have a great day."

Didi said goodbye and followed Luke outside to a station van. He opened the passenger door and cleaned off the seat. "Sorry. It's kind of messy in here. Been working by myself for a couple of weeks." He waited until she slid across the seat before closing her door. The interior smelled like a bag of cheese curls. Luke hopped into the driver's seat. "I read your bio. Never been to South Dakota, but I hear it's pretty."

"It's quite beautiful. I miss home. Where'd you grow up?"

He started the van and immediately, loud country music blared from the speakers. He pushed the button and silenced the radio. "Apologize for that. I like to jam. Me? I grew up in Columbia. My parents still live there."

"Oh. What state is Columbia in?"

He laughed and pointed south. "Right here in Pennsylvania. Along the river, down Route 441. It's actually our first stop."

Her mouth was suddenly dry. "Y-y-you're taking me to meet your parents?"

He laughed so hard he could barely buckle his seat belt. "Heavens no. The station wants video of you in front of the old Wrightsville-Columbia Bridge that's across the Susquehanna River, then we're heading to the Turkey Hill Experience for another photo op. If you want, we can get some ice cream there."

Didi stared out the window. She'd read his intentions completely wrong. *I'm messing this up.* But Luke didn't seem to notice.

"I understand you're new here, so let me give you the grand tour." For the next forty-five minutes, he kept up a rolling commentary about the local towns and history of the area. Luke made the ride quite interesting. After descending the large hill that overlooked Columbia, he parked the van near the railroad tracks that ran along the Susquehanna River. Fat raindrops suddenly exploded on the windshield. Didi reached for the door handle, but Luke's voice stopped her. "Hold up a second. It's my responsibility to make sure you always look your best. Please don't get out of the vehicle when the weather's bad. Just wait for me."

What? In a few seconds, he appeared with a large umbrella emblazoned with the station logo. He opened her door and held the rain screen above her. He was getting soaked, but made sure she was dry. Didi stared at him. "Want to share this with me?"

He shook his head. "Nope. You're the important one." He retrieved his camera and covered it in plastic, then led her toward the river.

Didi pointed to the little islands which were in a line next to the Art Deco roadway. "What are those?"

The rain was coming down hard, splashing up against her calves. The cameraman didn't seem to notice as he wiped water from his face. "During the civil war, there was a wooden bridge across this river. Those islands are the remnants. When the Confederates came to Wrightsville over there," he pointed across the water, "the Union Army burned it down. Those soldiers actually saved the nation that day. If the rebels would have made it to this side of the bridge, they'd have won the war."

While history wasn't her best subject, Didi didn't remember hearing this before. "Why do you say that?"

Luke pointed north along the banks. "Clear shot to Harrisburg. Ninety percent of the Federal army's ammunition and one hundred percent of the coal for the Union navy came through Pennsylvania's capital. Even if General Lee would have held it for a single week, it would have kept the Union from waging war. Abe Lincoln would have had to surrender." He raised the camera. "Okay, Didi. Give me your best smile and turn the umbrella so I can see the station logo."

It continued to rain for the rest of the day and each time they stopped, Luke made sure to keep her dry. They returned to the station a little after five. He held the door for her, his sneakers squishing water out of the laces as they sauntered down the terrazzo-lined hall. "I've got to upload the video, so I'll say good night. Rest up and I'll see you here at four tomorrow."

Her chin trembled. "Why so early?"

He smiled and for the first time, she noted how white his teeth were. "Oh, they didn't tell you? You're one of the morning reporters. Hope you had a good day today." He winked at her. "I sure did." And just like that, he turned and walked off.

Didi muttered under her breath. She certainly wasn't looking forward to the early arrival, but she *was* looking forward to working with Luke.

***

Riley smiled at the man who opened her door. Even though Mick lived and worked in Philly, he visited her at least twice a week. Since she worked from three until midnight, mornings were when they got together.

His grin was goofy today. "You be hungry?"

"A little, eh?" she teased.

His hand was warm when he offered it. Riley could feel his strength, and how he always held back a little when he touched her. *Like he's holding a china doll.* And like the gentleman he was, he opened the door for her at Miller's Smorgasbord.

"I appreciate you taking time to always come up to see me. Maybe sometime I could come visit you. Maybe watch you work out."

He eyed her strangely. "Dis be as a reporter or as my girl?"

Riley's chest tingled. "Am I your girl?"

The big man's face turned pink. "Duh, well yeah. At least I be thinkin' so. Dat okay?"

From the warmth of her face, she realized she was blushing. "Yes. I-I really like that idea."

"Me, too." As always, Mick talked non-stop. He had so many funny stories, many of which were about the pranks he pulled on other players on the team. "You know Rocco, the backup goalie?"

Riley could get lost in his eyes. "Um-huh?"

A young boy walked over and asked for Mick's autograph. He signed it, then posed with the youth as the mother took a snapshot. Mick continued as if he hadn't stopped. "Last week, I put ink on da headband of dis guy's helmet. Mustn't a been noticed. When he took it off, he had dis black line across his forehead. The team really busted his chops about it. They call him da 'streak' now, eh?"

Riley touched his hand. "You really love hockey, don't you?"

He nodded. "Yeah, it be hard work though, stayin' in tip-top shape."

The reporter in her surfaced. "So what's a typical day like for you?"

He took a bite of his omelet and smiled until he swallowed. "Hit da ice about six. Warm-up skate for twenty minutes, den I do wind skates, fifty of 'em, up and down the ice."

"Wind skates?"

"Yeah, you know, goin' as fast as I can. Keeps me in shape. Then I hit the exercise room for an hour. By dat time, everybody else shows up and we all practice."

"You do that by yourself? Why?"

He flexed his massive bicep. "Dese don't grow on trees, ya' know?"

Riley suppressed a giggle. "You do that every day?"

"'Cepting when I come to see you." His laugh lines seemed to fade. "I hope you know, Riley Espenshade, you be important to me. Maybe more den da sport itself."

She had to look away momentarily. This relationship was going much faster than she'd dreamed possible. "You're special to me, too, Mick."

His smile returned. "I kinda got dat. Hey, whatcha be doin' Sunday morning?"

"I-I don't know. Probably church. Have something in mind?"

"Yep. Ashley and Harry are visitin' the kids up in da cancer ward in Hershey. Asked me to tag along. I be hopin' you go wid me, eh?"

"S-sure, but why are you going?"

His perpetual smile faded. "Ashley had da cancer, when she be young."

I remember. "Okay. So?"

"Somethin' my daddy told me when I be little. He said, 'Now, Mikey'... he calls me Mikey, ya know? He said, 'Mikey, da Man above made you big for a reason, boy. You be strong and da strong always take care of da weak.' Dis be my way of helpin' da kids. My heart goes out to 'em. When I met Ashley, I thought she be so frail. And den when she told me she had the cancer, not once but twice, it made me sad." He balled his fist and concentrated on his drink. "I wish dat cancer was a man. I'd beat him to death. Since he ain't, I just do what I can." He paused and drained his coffee cup. His eyes met hers. "Riley, dis be important to me, and... and I want you to be part of dis wid me, okay?"

The look on his face made her heart swell. This man before her was a sports legend, yet he was unlike any star—or other man for that matter—that she'd ever met. She reached across the table and held his hand. Her voice was but a whisper. "I'd love that."

Mick suddenly stood and lifted her from her seat into his arms. His lips were so close. "I knew when I saw you, you weren't just no pretty face. You got a pretty heart. So happy you be my girl."

Riley touched his face. "Me, too." He lowered his lips toward hers. Riley met him halfway. *You've got a pretty heart, too. Eh?*

Chapter 4

T he bell on the door jingled as Didi swung it open. The heavenly scents commingled, creating a wonderful palette of aromas— Dutch apple pie, pumpkin rolls, chocolate cake, cookies... Didi's eyes closed as the wondrous bouquet filled her head.

The woman's greeting interrupted the delectable thoughts. "Hey! I haven't seen you for a while. How have you been?" Hannah slipped out of her apron, walked from behind the counter and pulled Didi into a strong hug. "Are you enjoying the new job?"

Didi held on to her tightly for a few extended seconds. "It's okay. Beats sitting in the Traffax Command Center, like I did all the time in Cleveland." Both women giggled. "This is such a pretty area."

Hannah studied her face briefly. "It is. Say, would you like a cup of coffee?"

There was nothing Didi wanted more than a long talk with someone. "You certain? I caught you in the middle of working, and I don't want to interrupt."

Hannah laughed. "I'm done baking for the day and besides, afternoon's the slow time. It'll pick up about three and be busy until I close at five. Decaf or regular?"

Didi walked around the showroom, checking out the décor. "Decaf, please. With the early hours, I'm usually in bed by six-thirty."

Hannah's voice flowed between the swinging doors separating the showroom from the kitchen. "Doesn't sound like fun. Cream or sugar?"

"Just cream, if you don't mind." The worst part of this job was the solitude. Even though she lived with Riley, they were like two ships passing in the night. Riley left for work at two in the afternoon. Didi didn't arrive home much before one-thirty. *I hate being alone.* A framed picture on the wall drew her attention. From their wedding. Hannah looked so beautiful in her wedding gown. And Sam? So happy, sporting that crooked smile Didi loved. She reached up to touch his face.

"That day was my all-time favorite. Glad you were there to share it with us."

It was like someone poured boiling hot wax on her. *Hannah caught me looking at Sam.* It was suddenly extremely warm. "I, uh, was just, uh... remembering your wedding."

Hannah's face sported a frown. "You okay? Your face is all red, like you're overheated. Maybe I should get you something cold to drink instead." Hannah placed the two coffee cups and the container of cream on a small wooden table. Two chocolate whoopee pies were already there.

Didi's hands trembled as she poured the cream. *Does Hannah know?*

Hannah sat next to her. "What's wrong, Didi?"

26

I'm really attracted to your husband. "I-I, uh, I don't know."

Hannah shook her head and laughed. "Didi, like Riley said, we're family. Tell me what's wrong. I'll help you if I can."

Didi swallowed hard as she gauged Sam's wife. The woman was so confident, and happiness seemed to flow from her. *I'd be happy too, if Sam loved me.* "I'm desperately lonely. I never see anyone, except at work. I eat alone, I work out alone, and watch TV alone. I thought Riley and I would be working the same shift. Maybe I made a mistake coming here."

Hannah handed her the chocolate treat. "Here, kiddo. Chocolate always helps. Let's handle this one problem at a time. Why don't you come over for supper a couple times a week? Beth idolizes you. I know she'd love that."

Didi shook her head. "I don't want to take away from family time." She took a bite of the wonderful pastry. It melted in her mouth. "This is delicious. Did you make it?"

"Of course. After all, we have a bakery." Hannah laughed. "And don't worry about family time. With our work schedule, we make time when we can. Sam spends all day selling our wares at the markets on Tuesdays and Fridays, plus half a day Saturday. We'd be happy to have you eat with us."

Didi washed the treat down with coffee. "Can you show me how to make these?"

The warmth of Hannah's smile calmed Didi's fears. "I'd love to." The older woman waited until she caught Didi's eyes. "I meant what I said. You're family now. You can spend time here with me every day, if you want."

"Y-you wouldn't mind? You sure?"

"Absolutely."

Didi jumped up and hugged her new friend. "You're the best, Hannah." As Hannah patted her back, Didi's eyes again gravitated to the wedding photo, and Sam. *You're the best.*

***

Riley slid into the booth across from Harry and Ashley Campbell. Mick forced himself in next to her. She couldn't help but snicker at him when he motioned to the waitress. "Got a table wid real chairs? Dis booth, it be a little tight for me."

The waitress obliged and Riley could sense Mick's relief.

The big guy turned to Ashley. "So how's dis goin' down? Whatcha want me to do?"

The petite blonde with thick hair replied quickly. "The nurses introduce us, then Harry will read to them." She turned to Riley. "Did you know my Harry writes kid's books?"

"No. How cool!" Riley saw Harry turn bright red.

Ashley was beaming. "He's working on a series about kids fighting cancer."

Harry nodded. "In Princess's honor. Wish I would have been there when she was younger."

It was Ashley's turn to blush. The back of her fingers lightly brushed against her husband's face. "But you're with me now. I love you so much, Harry."

Harry stood and lifted Ashley into his arms. The pair shared a long kiss.

Riley glanced at Mick. He was smiling and had a dreamy expression. *I love his eyes.*

The hockey star cleared his throat. "Don't know if you be noticin', but we be here, too."

The pair sat back down. Ashley continued, "Sorry. We were just hoping you would kind of like hang with the kids. It's so cool to have a big sports star around."

Mick smiled. "Glad ta help. And don't forget, we be havin' a television star here too, eh?" He reached across and squeezed Riley's hand. "She be real important, 'specially ta me."

Riley's face heated. *What did I get myself into?*

***

Mick sat, a sick kid on each knee. He was just as entranced as the children were with Harry's story, and how Ashley and Harry both read the book. It was plain to see they were in love. His gaze drifted to Riley, holding a bareheaded little girl on her lap. *In love, just like me.*

The Campbells finished the book and pulled out another. Mick caught Riley's gaze. When she noticed him looking at her, she smiled and then whispered, "Thank you for asking me to come, to share this with you."

He nodded at the child in her arms. "You be lookin' like a natural. Holdin' that little girl."

"She's precious, isn't she?" The little girl was sucking her thumb, snuggled into Riley's arms.

29

His mind wandered and a vision appeared. Of him and Riley holding that little girl. Taking care of her. Protecting her from the pain evident in her eyes. Being a family.

"Yes, she's treasured by all of us here," a voice said. Mick turned to find a nurse smiling at the little girl. "This is Molly. Poor child, she's an orphan. Her mother passed away a couple of months ago. Died of liver cancer. The little girl doesn't have anyone but us."

Mick handed the little ones who were on his knees back to their mothers. His eyes grew blurry. *I hate you, cancer.* "What about her dad?"

The nurse touched the girl's face. "He was never in her life."

Mick reached to Riley. "Let me hold her." Riley passed the child to him. He cradled the girl in his arms. "Hey der, Molly. I'm Mick." The little one's eyes took him in, her hand rubbing his chin. *The strong always take care of the weak.* He directed his voice to the nurse. "No one wants t'adopt her?"

The nurse wiped her cheeks. "Who would want to adopt a sick child that probably won't make it?"

Mick's nose tingled. "S'not right." A quiet voice whispered from his soul, *"Then you adopt her."* He softly kissed Molly's forehead. The little girl hugged him.

Riley touched his cheek. "Now who's the natural?"

He studied Riley's eyes. So soft, so vibrant. *Everything I could want, it be in my reach, right now.*

***

"That's a wrap. Great job, Didi." Luke's smile was wide and happy.

Didi turned off the microphone. "You're always so complimentary." *Because you like me?* She hoped so. Over the last couple of weeks, Luke had treated her like royalty. She knew he did things to make her shine, more so than any other camera person. At least that was what Riley said.

"We've got time. Like to grab a bite before we head back to the station?"

Didi's heart pushed her onward. "Maybe we could do dinner instead? I'll treat."

He studied her and his face seemed to glow. But just as quickly, his smile disappeared. "My unit's getting together tonight." Luke told her his National Guard unit was tight. His smile reappeared. "Want to come? I mean, everyone brings their families."

Like as his date? "What time?"

"We get together at seven. It usually breaks up around nine-thirty. Everyone would be thrilled to meet you."

Her mouth fell open as she turned to him. "Why would they want to meet me?"

Luke seemed to struggle on his response. "Uh, all the guys, well, they like watching you on the news. Everyone says how pretty you are."

Her cheeks warmed. "I... I don't know. We work tomorrow. Um... how about a raincheck on dinner?"

"Sure. Tomorrow night?"

She had a standing Friday night engagement. "I can't. I have plans."

Luke winced and looked away. "I understand. Hope you have fun on your date."

Didi touched his arm. "I'm having dinner with Hannah and her girls."

"Hannah?"

"Oh, sorry. Hannah is Riley's sister-in-law. Maybe you could eat with us?"

His frown grew. "I wouldn't want to intrude. How about Saturday or Sunday night?"

She shook her head. "I'm filling in for the evening anchor spot this weekend."

"I see..."

Didi could almost feel his sorrow. "We could do breakfast, but only if you want to."

His excitement was hard to hide. "Eden Resort does a Sunday brunch. Would that be okay?"

Her limbs tingled. "On one condition."

"That would be..."

She pointed at his shirt. "Wear something different. I think you've worn Luke Bryan shirts every day. You must really like him."

Luke tried to hide his grin, but failed. "I wear them because Bryan is my middle name. Luke Bryan Zinn."

Didi shook her head and laughed. "You're lying."

His smile was in full force now. "And here, I thought you trusted me."

"Really?" *I do. Totally.*

Chapter 5

D idi wrapped the last oatmeal whoopee pie in plastic and stacked it on the tray. *Can't believe I made these.* Hannah patted her back. "How scrumptious. If you keep this up, you'll be running the bakery soon."

A smile graced Didi's lips. Hannah had become the sister Didi never had. Every Tuesday and Friday, Hannah took the time to teach her how to bake. More importantly, how to be a true friend. And because of their closeness, Didi made sure not to be around when Sam was there. Didi wouldn't dare risk allowing anyone to see how she cared for Hannah's husband. Sam Espenshade was her Achilles heel.

"I forgot to ask, how is Mr. Luke Bryan these days?"

Luke. Her heart warmed as she thought of him. "I guess he's okay. I filled in for the morning traffic anchor all week and didn't get a chance to see much of him."

Hannah was cleaning the glass display case. "Seems like you two really hit it off, I mean with the brunch date going so well."

Didi's eyes closed and the vision of Luke, dressed in a gray pinstripe suit that Sunday morning swelled her heart. *Our date was pure magic.* "We did. I was hoping he would ask me out again, but so far he hasn't."

"He does know tomorrow's your birthday, doesn't he?"

She shrugged. "I dunno. Doesn't make a difference. He has guard duty this weekend."

"Sorry. I'd like to remind you though, tomorrow is also Saturday." Every Saturday morning, Didi, Hannah and her girls had breakfast tea at the Essence of Tuscany Tea Room. "I know it's not much, but we'll celebrate with you. And don't forget that you, Riley and I have plans to go shopping in the afternoon."

Didi turned. "Thank you for being so kind to me. For being my friend, for, for making my life less lonely."

Hannah laughed. "I think I've got the better end of the deal. I mean, you do a lot of the baking these days." Hannah sighed. "I'll go clean up. Mind tending the counter?"

"Sure." Hannah walked into the kitchen while Didi slid the tray of treats into the display case. The bell on the door tinkled.

"May I help…" Didi stopped mid-sentence. There before her, dressed in boots and fatigues and wearing his beret, was Luke Zinn. Her heart almost skipped a beat as she took in this handsome soldier.

He removed the cap and nodded. "Good afternoon, Ms. Phillips. Wanted to tell you something. I hope you know I missed you terribly this week."

Didi's hands trembled. "I missed you, too." She swallowed hard to chase away the butterflies. "How'd you know I was here?"

"I asked Ms. Espenshade where to find you."

"And, and you stopped in just to tell me you missed me?"

His smile started to melt her heart. "That was only part of the reason."

"Part? Why else?"

"To give you this." He handed her an envelope. "Open it."

She pulled the flap and removed the card. As she did, dozens of glittery confetti hearts fell to the floor. Didi's hands were shaking so badly she had trouble holding the paper. The birthday card was beautiful, but the handwritten note made her eyes watery.

Dearest Deidre, (my Didi),

I just wanted to take a moment to thank you for coming into my life. Since I met you, my whole world has changed. I feel like the luckiest man in the universe, not only to be the one fortunate enough to capture your image for eternity, but to spend time with you. I want you to know your smile will forever fill my heart, and also my dreams. I wish for you, on your birthday, a day filled with wonder, and hope you will be as happy as you make me. I'm sorry I can't celebrate it with you, but know my heart will be with you, always. And my birthday gift for you is the promise of a romantic date, anytime and anywhere, when we're on the road next week. My secret desire is that this is only the first of many birthdays we'll spend together. Happy Birthday, my most cherished friend.

Love, Luke (Bryan) Zinn

She stared at him, standing there with his beret in his hands. "I-I don't know what to say. Th-thank you?"

He nodded, then walked behind the counter and hugged her. She wrapped her arms around him. *This feels so good, so natural. I never want to let go.*

He slowly pulled away. "I hope this didn't come as a shock, but I can't hide the way I feel about you anymore." His lips brushed her hair. He stood tall. "Gotta go now. Have a long drive to Fort Indiantown Gap. Bye, Didi. Happy birthday." Luke squeezed her hands tightly, then turned and headed for the door.

Don't go! "Wait." His romantic gesture floored her and she was having trouble keeping her feelings inside. She grabbed a sack and started stuffing it with oatmeal whoopee pies. "I, uh, made these. Let me send some along for you, and, you know, for the guys, too."

His mouth dropped open. "You made these?"

She nodded vigorously. "Yes."

The way his eyes engaged her made her knees weak. "You do realize, if you send these along, you'll never see me alive again."

The sack dropped to the floor. "What?"

He laughed and leaned over to pick up the container. "The whole unit is already jealous because I get to spend my days with the most gorgeous girl in the world. When they find out you can bake, too, they'll kill me off in hopes they can take my place." He touched her face. "I hope you know I think the world of you, Deeds."

"D-Deeds?"

"Yep. That's how I think of you. Like every good deed imaginable, all rolled up in you." He took her hand and kissed her fingers. "Goodbye, my friend." And with that, he turned and left the shop.

Didi had to grab the counter to keep from falling over. *Am I hallucinating?*

A touch on her shoulder startled her. It was Hannah. "Everything all right?" Hannah noticed the glittery hearts on the floor. "What happened here?"

Didi grabbed her friend's arms. "Pinch me, quick."

Hannah laughed. "Why?"

"I think I died and went to heaven."

***

Mick kept his torso low as he flew down the ice. Just before reaching the boards, he slammed on the brakes, ice crystals flying as his skates bit in. He repeated the process in a fluid motion, traversing the length of the rink again. His eyes were blind to everything in the arena because all he saw were two faces, and they belonged to Riley and Molly. *There be my future, but the timin', it ain't right.* He loved playing hockey, but if he followed the voices in his head, he'd have to change, maybe even quit hockey. The voice whispered again, "*Anythin' worth doin', it need to be done right.*"

A sound drew his attention and he slowed. It was the coach. "I hope you save some of that energy for the game tonight."

"Don't you be worryin' 'bout me none. I be ready when da puck drops." Mick's entire body tingled from the tension of his thoughts.

The man studied him. "There something you want to tell me?"

"Don't think so. Why?"

"Because in all my years, I've never seen any player with your determination, your intensity. But in the last two weeks, the fire in your eyes is like an inferno. If I was lined up against you, I'd fear for my life. What's going on?"

Not knowin' how to solve my problem. "Like I said, nothin'. Want me ta back down a notch?"

The coach shook his head. "Hell no. You're on fire, boy. A hat trick in each of the last four games? Wish I could bottle up your zeal. I'd make a billion dollars off it."

The stress was again building in Mick's arms. *Need to keep skatin'.* "If'n der's nothin' else you be wantin', I be gettin' back to my workout. I need da exercise."

"Damn, Mick. Wish I could clone you. Got an hour before the team practice."

"Aye. I be ready." Mick nodded and pushed off. The battle between his heart and his mind raged on with fierce intensity. His daddy's words echoed through his head. *"The strong always protect the weak."* His heart chipped in. *Molly needs both you and Riley.* The image of the ice faded and a vision filled him. He and Riley were holding the little girl.

To do dis right, I might just need to be givin' up hockey. The struggle continued as he pushed his body further, sweat running like a stream down his face. *But I love da game.*

The Zamboni drove onto the ice and Mick stopped in the middle of the rink. His eyes saw his "family." The thoughts in his head escaped his lips. "I be in love wid you, Riley Espenshade. An' I want ta be a father to Molly, and you, her momma. Us together, ya know? But I ain't ready to give up da sport." And if he mentioned his feelings, what would Riley say? He hoped she felt like he did, but who was he to know? "My heart wants things dat I can't have right now."

Mick skated to the opening to the locker room. He cast one last glance at the ice, but it was Riley's vision before him. Sporting her beautiful smile. "What would you say if I told ya what be on my mind, eh?" Maybe it was time to ask her.

Chapter 6

C old rain continued to fall, soaking every piece of clothing he wore. Kyle Parker shivered as he watched the Espenshade home. Lights flickered off in the northernmost corner of the second floor. "And that would be Beth's room." Since his release from the county prison, Kyle had been monitoring the homes of both Hannah Espenshade and Henry Campbell. Kyle's time in prison had not been fun. *You two are the reason I got in trouble. Gettin' me fired just started the ball rolling.*

Kyle rolled onto his side and noted the time in his log book. "When I pay you back, Hannah, you'll remember it... for the rest of your life." He wrapped the rubber band around the journal and returned it to his backpack. Kyle quietly slipped off into the night.

***

Riley pushed the plate back from her chair at the breakfast table. "That was tasty, Hannah."

Her sister-in-law smiled. "Sure you don't want more?"

Riley rubbed a hand against her smooth stomach. "There's a difference between wanting more and eating more. I have an image to uphold, or at least control. I don't understand how you stay so trim."

Hannah laughed. "Wait until you have three kids to chase around. You'll understand."

She's pregnant? Riley's eyes went wide. "Are you and Sam expecting already?"

Hannah shook her head. "I was referring to your brother. Sometimes it feels like I have three children."

Riley laughed. "I understand. Don't forget he was my roomie in Cleveland for three months." A vision of his smile filled her mind. Her brother had confided he and Hannah decided to have a baby just months after the wedding. After he'd first asked Hannah's two girls if they would mind. And the girls were ecstatic. The closeness of this family made her wish... Well, not just yet. *I want to establish myself as a premier sportscaster, before...*

Hannah grabbed the dishes and carried them to the kitchen. Riley followed. "So how's it going between you and Mickey?" The older lady turned and Riley could see the devilment in her eyes. "He's quite a catch, you know? So tall and handsome. Not to mention the way he acts whenever he's around you. You do realize, Mickey is head over heels in love with you, don't you?"

Riley's face warmed. "Yes. He's told me that, several times."

"And is that how you feel?"

Riley nodded. "Maybe." She waited until Hannah looked at her. "Do you think we're going too fast?"

Hannah shrugged. "Each couple is different."

"When did you and Sam fall in love?"

The smile on Sam's wife's face was gentle. "I think Sam fell in love with me that day we met, at the picnic. It took me a while longer. In fact, I think both my daughters realized they loved him before I did. But when Sam came over to take care of me, you know, after the bull kicked me... that's when I finally knew. Admitting that to myself was quite a shock, actually. It took us both a while to say it to each other."

She was spot on. *Sam had fallen in love with Hannah that first day.* "But you guys worked out your issues and now look at you two, poster kids for true love."

Hannah was blushing now. "Getting back to the two of you... "

Riley drew a deep breath. "I think it started at Ashley's wedding. But I've been hurt before and especially because he's a professional athlete... There are busloads of women who'd give anything to take my spot. Hannah, I'm a little scared."

Hannah touched her arm. "But Mickey's only interested in you, isn't he?"

She nodded. "Yes. He's made that plain. And I love being with him, but Hannah, with his schedule, it's hard sometimes."

Hannah went back to loading the dishwasher. "Life has a way of working out the details. Speaking from experience, even when you aren't ready, God prods you along."

That's odd. "What do you mean?"

Hannah smiled. "I had no plans on ever trusting someone totally, ever. Especially not a boy twelve years younger. But what happened between us... " Hannah moved until they were face to face. "It was magic. I don't know how to express it any other way."

Riley turned, suddenly uncomfortable with the conversation. *I'm just not ready.* She took the opportunity to change the subject. "I hear from Didi that the two of you are close. She told me she thinks of you like the sister she never had." Riley noticed the funny grin on her sister-in-law's face. "I was surprised, especially since I told you how she feels about your husband."

Hannah giggled. "Yes, it's strange, isn't it? Remember the old adage, keep your friends close, but your enemies closer?"

"Um-hmm."

Hannah's face softened. "That's why I was nice at first, but Didi's a great kid. We've actually become close friends. The girl makes sure she's never here when Sam's home. Maybe it's a coping mechanism, but I think it's out of respect. Besides, Didi's entranced with Mr. Luke Bryan Zinn now."

Riley shook her head. "Bryan isn't his real middle name. He's teasing Didi."

Hannah nodded. "I'm pretty sure she knows and even surer it doesn't matter." Hannah studied her. "Nice try to change the subject. How do you really feel about the hockey star?"

Riley's mouth was dry. *I'm trying to sort that out.* She glanced at her watch. "Oh, look at the time. I've got to get home and get ready for work. We'll continue this later. Bye."

Her sister-in-law hugged her. "Whatever you say, but the answer's on your face. Just remember to listen to your heart."

Riley retreated to her Escape. *If I listen to my heart, I'll have to give up my dreams.*

Chapter 7

Luke's hand trembled as he loaded his equipment into the new SUV the station assigned to him. When he'd seen her inside the studio this morning, the blonde looked even more beautiful than he could ever remember. He thought of his visit last week. And the romantic note he'd written in the card. *Such a fool.* The look of confusion on her face when she'd read it told him everything. *I'm nothing.* He was glad... kind of... that they had Monday off. *What would she ever see in me?*

Didi approached, a smile lighting her face. He quickly moved to hold open her car door before sliding into the driver's seat. *What should I say?*

Before he could break the ice, her sweet voice reached his ears. "Did you have a good weekend? I was hoping you'd call yesterday, so we could do something together. I didn't want to phone you because I wasn't sure how long your Guard obligations were."

Luke had to be careful not to move his foot because his jaw was on the floor and he was afraid he'd step on it. *Am I dreaming?* It was a few moments before he could answer. "I, uh, well, uh, I-

I...w-wasn't quite sure how you took my card... and the note."

She softly touched his hand. Hers was trembling. "Your card was the best birthday present I ever received." Blush colored her face. "I'm not too good at this, so, if I mess this up, please forgive me." Didi hesitated, then whispered, "I'm hoping your last line comes true."

What the heck did I write last? "What line?"

For the first time, he noticed the depth of her eyes. Of course he knew they were blue, but the sea blue hue seemed to go on forever. "The part about this only being the first of many birthdays we'll spend together." She swallowed, hard. "I really like you, too."

His whole body relaxed. "So, it's not just me?"

"No... " Didi's hand moved toward his cheek. The electricity of her closeness sent shivers of pleasure through his body. But before her fingers reached his skin, there was a loud knock on the window. Even in the light from the interior lamps, he noted her face turn white. Didi wound down the window. "Yes?" she said to one of the other morning reporters.

The man handed her a cup. "You left your coffee inside. Knowing how mornings are, I thought you might want it."

She took the drink container. "Thanks. Have a great day." Didi closed the window and turned to Luke. Her complexion was still quite pale. "I'd like to continue our conversation, but probably not while we're working. Is that okay?"

Luke nodded. "Agreed. Our first stop today is in Willow Street. I'll drive."

The girl giggled. "Excellent idea. Especially since you're in the driver's seat."

Luke's cheeks heated. "By the way, you look lovely today."

Didi flashed him a wholesome smile. "Thank you." He couldn't help but gaze at her. The width of her smile increased. "Maybe we should get going?"

"I agree."

Didi laughed. "I'm not the one in the driver's seat. You are."

Luke shook his head to break the trance. "You're right." He turned the ignition switch and put the vehicle in drive. *Please don't let this be a dream.*

***

Henry Campbell stood at the edge of the field, his brother Edmund beside him. "I see what you mean. This was intentional." Henry examined the mutilated butternut squash. "Clean cut, once through. No serrations. My guess would be the damage came from a machete."

Edmund stared at his brother. "Did you notice it's just these squash? The ones of highest value, no less. Fortunately, it's only about a hundred or so and not all of them."

Henry chucked the split vegetable to the side and walked the pumpkin patch.

His younger brother followed along. "What are you looking for?"

Henry crouched down. "These." He waited until Edmund was next to him. "See the boot marks?" He retrieved his cell and snapped an image. "I'll walk down to the end of the row. You start here. Take pictures of every one of these you find."

Edmund stood. "Okay, but why?"

"Just a hunch. If we find multiple imprints, it was probably just some kids getting rowdy. If not, then we know this was an intentional attack against us."

Their search revealed two different sized marks. Henry examined them. "Similar shoe types, but one is much larger."

"What do you want to do?"

Henry stood, surveying the area. "Nothing right now. I'll go back and document it, in case it happens again. But I want to walk back to the office instead of hitching a ride with you. Need some time to think. See you later."

After Edmund left, Henry found what he was looking for—tire tracks, as if someone had pulled a car off the road. He shook his head. He had a hunch who was responsible. Someone who had been released from jail a couple of weeks ago. *If I find out this was you, Kyle Parker, you're going to face my wrath, again. And this time I won't play nice.*

***

Luke held the door for his newscaster, happiness filling his heart. Even though they were working, he'd never had a better day. *Being with her is absolutely perfect.* It was a little after one when he and Didi entered the building, observing the hustle and bustle of Roots Market. Didi was so different than any other reporter he'd ever worked with. She always waited for him to walk next to her, not behind her. His beautiful companion always asked his opinion, making him feel important.

She stopped, turned to him and smiled. "Do you have any specific stand in mind?"

"Nope. Lady's choice."

He noted the slight blush on her cheeks as she responded, "Well then, let's head over here."

She took off through the market and he followed. *That's odd. She didn't wait for me.*

Didi finally led him to a stand offering baked goods. He recognized the sign above the table. It was the same logo that had been on the door of the bakery where he'd found her last Friday. A man was waiting on a customer. The stand operator moved with a cane, which struck Luke as odd because of the gentleman's age.

While Didi spoke to the attendant, Luke checked out his camera. When she nodded, he hoisted the device to his shoulder. "Ready when you are, Didi." He focused the lens so he could capture her report.

"Today, we're continuing our coverage of South Central Pennsylvania's fall sweet spots. This is Didi Phillips, and today we're at Roots Country Market and Auction. I'm standing in front of the stand for Hannah's Bakery." She turned and motioned for the cashier to approach. "This is Sam Espenshade, one of the owners. The name might sound familiar to viewers and it should. Sam is the younger brother of our evening sports reporter, Riley Espenshade. Sam, tell us about what you have here."

A strange feeling gnawed at Luke as he watched the interaction between Didi and her interviewee.

They know each other. Of course they would. He'd heard Didi shared an apartment with Riley. If he was Riley's brother, the two would be acquaintances. But what bothered him most was the intimate way the two interacted.

After the interview was finished, Didi gave Riley's brother a very long hug. A sinking feeling filled Luke. *They're lovers.* As his news reporter turned from the man, her face was bright red.

Didi's eyes didn't quite reach his. "I guess we should head back to the station."

Luke's hands and arms were shaking. "Let's pick another stand to spotlight."

That beautiful face was now covered with a frown. "Why? Did I do something wrong?" She judged his face. "Are you jealous?"

That pretty much confirmed my suspicions. "Jealous? What's that mean?"

She pointed her finger at his face. "I saw the disapproval in your eyes during the interview."

Luke shook his head. "You misread me. It's getting late and we can talk about this some other time. We need to film another sequence because I'm pretty sure the station won't run the one we just did."

"Because of what you'll say. Why are you jealous of Sam?"

"Didi, this isn't the time or the place. And the reason has nothing to do with me."

"I don't believe you. I saw the look on your face."

"That's not it at all."

Her arms were on her hips and people were beginning to stare. *Great. Our first fight.* "Then why?"

"Because that's Riley's family. It's called nepotism."

Chapter 8

R iley planted a kiss on Mick's cheek. "It's good to see you." He looked so tired. "I appreciate you always coming to see me, but maybe you need a break." He held her door and she climbed in.

"I be fine. Kinda rough game last night. That be all."

Riley had seen the highlights. Her hockey player was on track to set a new all-time NHL scoring record, and because of that, he'd become the target for goons on every team. "I watched the film. You took a pretty hard shot to your ribs. Can't believe the refs missed that call. Does it hurt?"

He lifted his shirt. His whole right rib cage was black and blue. A large bandage had red splotches in the center. "Tink da top of his stick had a nail in it. Bled like a pig." A smile broke out across his face. "Paid him back. See it?"

She'd also seen the fight. Despite a two-on-one disadvantage, the mighty Campeau had easily prevailed. They had to carry his opponents off the ice after escorting Mick to the penalty box.

Riley lightly touched his face. "You've got to be more careful. I-I don't know what I'd do if you were seriously hurt. What precipitated the fight, when he stuck you in the ribs?"

He looked away. "No, what dey said."

"What was that?"

"Said nasty things. 'Bout you. Won't take dat."

She gently grasped his head and turned it to her. "It's just trash talk. They do that to get under your skin. You should learn to ignore it."

The man leaned in and softly kissed her lips. "No one calls my girl a tramp, ever. Told him da next time, I'd be breakin' his filthy neck, eh?"

"Mickey..."

He suddenly sat up straight and changed the subject. "Hungry? I be starvin'."

She knew there was no sense talking to this giant. "I am. Where are we going?"

"Bob Evans. Hershey."

"Why there?"

Color seeped into his cheeks. "Wanna see my other girl, you know?"

Her eyes opened wide, then narrowed. She felt the heat in her face. "Molly?"

He shifted his Jeep into drive and nodded. "Dat be da one."

Riley rolled her eyes. "Again? We visited her twice last week. I think you care more about her than you do me."

Mick slammed on the brakes and if she hadn't been wearing her seatbelt, she might have flown through the windshield. His large index finger was soft against the bottom of her chin. The look on his face was serious, yet sad. "You be gettin' this straight, Riley Espenshade. I be lovin' you more den life itself. Hopefully ya know that, eh?"

Riley wondered if she would melt right there on the spot. *Never more certain of anything else, ever.* She could only nod in response.

Sadness filled his eyes. "Ain't much, but you got me. Little Molly, she ain't got no one. No mama, no papa. Don't you dare be feelin' it's a competition. I love you, more den I could ever say. But my heart goes out to dat baby. Fightin' dat damned cancer all by herself. She be needin' us." He pawed his eyes with his ginormous hands. "Please don't be makin' me choose 'tween you 'n' her. Know you'd win, but it be makin' me real sad inside if'n you did."

The warmth of his love and compassion touched Riley. *He's a teddy bear.* Despite his size and rough ways, inside him was a heart of gold. She nodded. "You're right. Let's pay Molly a visit."

A smile lit up his face. "I brought her somethin'."

"What?"

"Got her one of dem cell phones."

Riley giggled. "She's only two years old... and besides, I've never heard her speak."

His eyes searched hers. "It's so we can Skype wid her. Ya know, for days we can't visit. I think she be enjoyin' dat."

Riley shook her head. "And here they said you were nothing but brawn and fists. You're a pussy cat inside, Michael Campeau."

He touched her nose. "No one but you need ta know it, 'kay?"

She reached over and kissed him. "Your secret's safe with me."

The swiftness of his hug startled her. "Love you so much. Knew when I saw your face, you was purty, inside and out."

A voice whispered to her. *This is where you belong.* For the first time, she admitted it out loud. Riley pulled back so he could see her eyes. "I love you, too." She hugged him and then whispered in his ear. "Eh?"

***

Didi stared out of the window. Luke turned onto a side road, heading toward Harrisburg. The last hour had not been at all what she'd hoped for. They needed to get this out in the open.

"I get the whole nepotism thing, but that's not what's wrong, is it?"

He stared through the windshield with vacant eyes. "Doesn't matter."

"I don't understand why you won't talk to me."

"You're a big girl, Didi."

"Thank you for noticing." She reached across to touch his hand. "You and I have never run out of things to say to each other. Before now."

He pulled away from her touch. "Guess we finally did."

She clenched her fists. "What happened to the man who gave me such a romantic card? I hope he reappears. If not, four days and nights on the road together are going to be pure misery."

"Then ask for a different camera man."

"Is that what you really want? I thought you liked me. Why should I request someone else?"

Silence greeted her. "Can you at least have the common courtesy to answer?"

He pulled the SUV to the side of the road. "You really want the truth?"

His expression concerned her, but they needed to discuss this. "Of course I do."

"Fine. Remember you asked for it." Luke drew a deep breath. "I don't want to be there to watch you self-destruct."

"What? I don't understand."

"Come on. You're smart, Didi. Probably the most intelligent woman I've ever met, but I refuse to watch you crash and burn. You hang around with that man's wife and live with his sister. There's no way this will end up good for you."

"You're talking about Sam? Of course I know he's married. Why would you..."

"You forget, I was there. The electricity between the two of you was enough to power a small city."

"Luke, I have no idea what you're talking about."

"The way you two acted. So intimate. I'm just a dumb hick, not college educated like you. But it was plain as the nose on my face."

Didi replayed the interview in her mind, but still didn't understand. Her anger started to boil over. "Then enlighten me, oh wise one." He shook his head and looked away. "What, you won't even tell me what you're thinking?"

Luke whipped around. "How long have you two been lovers?"

Didi's anger exploded into full blown madness. "Lovers? How dare you. I never slept with Sam or...

or any other man for that matter. Why would you even think that?"

His lips drew into a fine white line. "The way you two interacted. You mean to tell me there's nothing between you?"

"Did I stutter? The answer is no!"

"I don't believe you."

All restraint flew out the window. She slapped him. "How dare you judge me? You know what, I will ask for another camera man." He looked away, obvious hurt on his face. "And I thought you were someone special."

When they got back to the station, she followed as Luke raced in and beat his fist on the station manager's door until it flew open. The red-faced woman growled at him, "This better be important, Zinn. I was on a call with the network VP, until *you* interrupted."

"Find a replacement for this trip," Luke said. "I refuse to go anywhere with *her*."

Didi swallowed hard, willing the shaking to stop. The manager's glare was icy enough to freeze steam. "You interrupted me because the two of you are having a spat?" The boss shook her head violently and stuck her finger in Luke's face. "Get over it or clean out your desk."

Luke's mouth dropped open. "What?"

"Cameramen are a dime a dozen." The woman nodded in Didi's direction. "Reporters like her are priceless. Suck it up or go home permanently." She slammed the door in both their faces. Even standing outside her office, they could hear her rant, "Stupid idiot."

Luke whipped around to face Didi. His lips were moving, but no sound came out. Luke Bryan Zinn stormed off into the night.

***

Their SUV was headed northeast, toward Bushkill Falls. They hadn't spoken that morning when packing their luggage. Nor had Luke spoken to her all day, except when he absolutely had to, for work purposes.

The vehicle lurched to a stop. "We're here. I'll grab the camera."

Didi opened her door and waited for him to hoist his equipment. "How do I look?"

He didn't even bother to glance at her. "Like normal. The picture of true beauty." He turned and walked away. She struggled to keep her disappointment inside while they walked down the trail and stairs so she could report with the bridal falls as a background. Because they'd worked together for so long, their actions were automatic, although today she had to force herself to smile.

When she was finished, Luke nodded. "Great job, as always."

"Wow! The man actually can speak."

He shook his head. "Whatever."

Luke headed up the steep stairs in front of her. In anger, she stormed after him, twenty feet behind. She was ten slats up when she missed a tread, lost her balance and fell backwards.

Unable to catch herself, she landed on the platform and rolled through the gap between the platform and the railing. There was nothing between her and the rock at the bottom of the falls, maybe fifty feet below.

But her descent suddenly stopped. Pain screamed up her leg from her ankle. Her foot was caught on a piece of rope from the railing. She yelled out in agony.

"Didi! Hold on. I'm coming." She glanced back to the platform to see Luke leap over the railing and grab the post just before he could fall into the abyss. "Give me your hand."

It took all her strength, but she curled her body, hand extended. She glanced at the rope. *My foot's coming loose!* Their fingers barely touched, but Luke grasped her firmly and pulled Didi toward him.

"Grab ahold of me."

She obeyed immediately.

He released her hand and grabbed her under the arm. He lifted her up until her head was on his shoulder. "Hold tight. I'll untangle your foot and then we'll get you onto solid ground."

Didi swallowed hard, holding onto Luke for all she was worth as he freed her foot. Her leg, suddenly unanchored, flew down. *Nothing between me and the rocks.* Luke's strong arm wrapped around her waist for support.

"I'm scared, Luke."

"It's okay. I've got you, and I promise I'll never let you go. Release your grip and reach for the rail. Catch a firm hold, then pull yourself up."

She did as instructed and grabbed the railing.

When he seemed sure she had a firm grip, Luke released her waist and grabbed her upper leg. He pushed as she pulled. Didi squeezed between the rails and fell onto the wooden platform.

Her ankle was killing her, but Didi forced herself to stand, grabbing Luke's jacket as he climbed upward. Her arms were around him when he crested the wood and dropped to the platform. She landed on top of him, snug in his embrace.

He was trembling all over as he held her. To Didi's surprise, Luke pulled her closer into a very tight hug. "Please don't ever do anything like that again. I couldn't go on if something happened to you."

What? "T-Thank you. Are you all right?"

He clung to her with all his might, wetness from his cheeks on her face. "I am, now."

Chapter 9

The air in the hothouse was freezing cold. All of the ventilation windows were open and the night's deep frost had withered most of the cucumber vines. Henry Campbell turned to his brother. "Was there a malfunction in the controller? Why didn't the heaters come on?"

Edmund led him to the control panel. He pointed at the console. "This was intentional. Someone must have turned the switch to manual and forced the windows open."

"But the heaters should have cycled. Are we out of fuel?"

"I don't think so. Check this out." Edmund led his older brother outside to the electrical service panels. All of the disconnect switches were turned off. "The propane tanks are full. Someone shut off the power. And then, look at this." Edmund pointed to the monitoring box. "The communication monitor was turned to 'test'. It didn't send the alert message to our cell phones because it's in test mode." Edmund turned to face his brother. "Kyle Parker?"

Henry's arms quivered from anger. "I think so. I checked with the police after the incident with the squash. Kyle had an alibi. But that doesn't mean he didn't have someone else do it."

Edmund shook his head. "We need to talk to that arse."

Henry wiped his hands over his face. "Police gave me strict instructions not to approach Kyle. Apparently, he filed a restraining order against me."

"Then what the hell can we do? Should I go see him?" Henry shook his head. "Want to lock up all the electrical controls?"

"Can't do that. Got to have free access in case of an emergency. What do you think about surveillance cameras?"

"Quite an expense."

Henry patted his brother on the shoulder. "Do it. It will be cheaper than lawyer's fees if I get my hands on Kyle."

Edmund nodded. "Consider it done. Task one for today."

Henry watched Edmund walk away. "Messing with the business is one thing, Kyle, but if you hurt anyone in my family, nothing will keep me from getting to you. And when I do, God have mercy on your soul, because I won't. My family is everything to me."

***

"It's just starting to sink in, Mom. I could have died. Luke, he... he saved my life." Didi was sitting in the hotel bed, foot wrapped, elevated and on ice. "He carried me up all those stairs and rushed me to the hospital, despite him being hurt. If he hadn't rescued me, I wouldn't be alive."

A soft knock sounded from the door.

"It's him. Gotta go. Tell Daddy I love both of you. Goodbye." Her body tingled and butterflies filled her chest.

"Hello?"

The door started to open. "Can I come in, Didi?"

"Yes."

Luke entered, a pizza box and several plastic sacks in his hands. "I come bearing gifts." He stopped and stared for a moment. "Wow. How is this possible?"

Didi squeezed her fingers together so he wouldn't see them shaking. "What?"

His smile warmed her heart and soul. "Each time I see you, your beauty... it amazes me. You just keep getting prettier and prettier."

Didi's cheek's warmed. No one had ever made her feel this way or treated her with such kindness. "Thank you. How's your hand?" The emergency room physician had to surgically remove the five-inch sliver of wood from when Luke grabbed the splintered wooden post after he jumped over the railing. *When he saved my life.*

"I'm fine. How's the ankle?"

"Feels much better now. Thanks for re-wrapping it when we got here. Where'd you learn to do that?"

Luke laughed, igniting happiness in Didi. "My mom taught me. She's a nurse, you know? Someday, maybe I'll take you to meet her. And besides, the Guard trained me as a medic."

Did they teach you to be a super hero, too? "I-I don't know how to say thank you. For saving me, for carrying me to the car, for... for everything."

Luke's eyes clouded. "I was never more scared in my life. Seeing you dangling there. I, uh, I'm just glad you're all right, that's all." He took a deep breath. "Want some pizza? I had it made with half mushroom and half Italian sausage. And I brought some diet Pepsi."

My favorites. A mischievous feeling took over. "What? No dessert?"

He laughed. "Of course. Double Stuffed Oreos. And mint chocolate chip ice cream."

"They're like my weakness, but you knew that, didn't you?"

His smile turned into a smirk. "I'll admit I kinda did."

"If I didn't know better, Luke Bryan Zinn, I might think you liked me."

It was his turn to blush. "You know I do."

Didi suddenly felt guilty for teasing him. "You proved that today. I, uh..."

His brows furrowed. "Today was my fault. If I hadn't acted like a jerk, you would have been beside me, not behind me. I hope you can forgive me."

It was me, not you. "No, no, it was my fault. Should have been watching where I was going. Lucky that rope was there."

"About that. Did you see how the rope fell after I untangled your foot? It's almost like God placed it there, just to catch you."

Didi took a deep breath as she tried to force the horror of that moment away. "Maybe He did, but I'm pretty sure of something else, too. God intended for you to be there to save me. If you hadn't..." The emotion was too much.

Luke set everything aside and reached for her.

Didi grasped him tightly. "How can I ever repay you?"

Luke's response was immediate. "Tell me what's happening between you and Sam. I need to know, Didi. I gave my heart away once before, and, let's just say it didn't end well."

She wiped her cheeks. "Okay. I owe you complete honesty." Didi drew a deep breath and looked away, but before she spoke, she engaged Luke's dark brown eyes. "I met Sam when he was recuperating from his broken leg. He was staying with Riley in Cleveland. We became friends and I... I admit... I had a massive crush on him. Sam treated me kindly, but not as nice as you have. On Christmas Eve, I was really worried because I couldn't get hold of my parents and he took me in."

Luke cocked his head and his eyes widened. "Took you in?"

Didi touched his face. "Yes. I was looking for Riley, but she wasn't home. He allowed me to stay and we watched movies and talked. The moment felt right and, uh, he and I were about to kiss." She felt her own cheeks heat. "But Riley came home and broke it up before we did." Didi repositioned her sore leg. "He went back to Hannah the next day and they patched it up. Nobody had ever treated me as nice as he did."

Luke grimaced and started to get up. "I see."

Didi grabbed his hand. "Until you came along. I suspected, well... I hoped the way you were treating me wasn't just because we worked together. You have no idea how wonderful that card made me feel, Luke. Like my life was finally beginning."

She couldn't read the look on his face. "Let me make it plain for you. Sam holds a special place in my heart, but, but..." Her face was on fire. "He's not the one I want anymore." Didi grasped Luke's face in her hands. "It's you, and not because you saved me. I really care for you. I have for quite a while." She pulled him in until their lips were about to touch.

Suddenly, Luke pulled away. "Let's not get carried away. I really like you, too. But let me show you honor and respect first, please?"

Now she was confused. "Didn't you do that today?"

He nodded. "I tried to, but... because of what happened with Carter, I don't want to risk messing this up. Let's take our time. I think we might have something really special here. But Didi, I need to tell you something first."

Oh no. "Okay."

He turned beet red. "Don't think I'm a perv, but I was attracted to you long before we met."

That wasn't what I expected. "You were? When?"

The redness on his face increased. "When I found out you were coming to the station, I watched some of your reports and, well let's say I fell in love with, I, uh, mean I was taken by you, all of you, not just your pretty face." He sat on the edge of the bed and reached for her hand. His were so warm, so strong. "You don't know this, but I was always the sports camera man. I was slated to work with Riley, but I really, really wanted to be with you. I traded places with Monica, just so we could work together."

Didi's heart swelled. "I'm glad you did." Her face broke out into a wide smile. "You're special, Lucas Donald Zinn."

His eyes opened wide. "How'd you find out my middle name isn't Bryan?"

Didi laughed. "I'm a reporter, or did you forget? I get to the bottom of every story."

They had spoken earlier about watching a movie, but didn't get the chance. Instead, they talked and shared non-stop, all about their lives.

Didi was getting tired and tried to stifle a yawn. Luke noticed. "It's getting late. I should head to my room. Anything you need before I go? More ice? Tylenol?"

Didi's hands were trembling. Some of it was because he was close, but more was because of what had happened earlier, not to mention what she was about to say. "Would you stay with me tonight?"

Luke's mouth dropped open and he started to back away. "Didi..."

"I don't mean like that. You can sleep in the other bed. I-I don't want to be alone tonight. I need you to be with me."

Luke studied her. "Pretty rough day for you?"

"This afternoon was, but the rest of it was, well, kind of perfect. Hey, if you don't want to, I understand."

His warm hand touched her face. "Are you sure?"

She nodded. "Yes, I'd really like that."

He took a deep breath. "Okay. Let me get my bag from my room first."

She felt her cheeks heat. "This means a lot to me."

"Then it shall be done. Back real soon."

By the time he returned, she had shuffled to the bathroom and changed. Luke quickly dressed in gym shorts and a Luke Bryan tee shirt. He climbed into the other bed and reached for her hand. "Good night, Deeds."

"'Night, Luke." He reached up and turned off the light, but she could still see his face. The last thing she saw before she fell asleep was their hands, entwined over the gap between the beds. *Like we belong together...*

Chapter 10

Luke's mouth was dry as he pulled into the Tea Room lot. But it wasn't just his mouth. His chest was light and his arms tingled. The touch of her hand in his had him feeling things he'd never experienced before. Not even with Carter and they'd been engaged.

"You're trembling." Didi's words interrupted his thoughts. "We don't have to do this."

He exhaled through his nose. "I'm a man of my word." *Especially to you.* "You beat me fair and square, but you could've told me you were the county apple slingshot champion."

Didi giggled. *I love the way your eyes light up when you laugh.* "Maybe, but our deal was fair, and either way, we both got what we wanted. You meeting Hannah's family and me meeting your parents."

But Sam will be there. Luke drew a deep breath. "Okay. Let's get this over with." Since Didi and Luke were on the road Saturday, Didi had asked Hannah to postpone the weekend tea until Sunday. *This will be the test, how she reacts when she sees Sam.* He opened her door and offered his hand.

Didi slid out of the truck and pulled him close. "I know you're anxious and I know why."

"You do?"

"Um-hmm. You're concerned about Sam."

Did she read my mind or am I wearing my feelings on my sleeve? "Didi..."

The touch of her finger against his lips excited him. "It's my turn, now. Let me show *you* some honor and respect, like you've given me, okay?"

His breath didn't want to come out. "You don't need to."

"I want to. Shall we?"

He released her hand, but she immediately grasped his. They walked to the door, fingers entwined. The bell jingled when he opened it for her. A middle aged lady turned from her podium, smiled and reached for Didi. The young blonde hugged the woman, but didn't let go of Luke's hand. "So great to see you again, Didi."

"You, too. Jessica Snyder, this is my dearest friend, Luke Zinn."

The woman winked at him. "So I finally get to meet the real Luke Bryan, uh... I mean Zinn. I've heard a lot about you." She turned her attention back to his friend. "The Espenshades saved space at their table for the two of you. Back in the corner."

Didi led the way. Luke whispered, "Luke *Bryan* Zinn? Heard a lot about me?"

His girl winked. "I confessed I was hopeful. I told everyone all about you."

Before he could respond, they were at the table where Sam Espenshade was seated. The woman to his left had long strawberry blonde hair and was very pretty. A cute teenager and a young child were there, also. The little girl's face lit up when she caught sight of Didi. "Dee-bee!" She ran to Didi and hugged her legs. Didi kissed the girl's head. The little one's smile was enormous. "Look-it. See my button? I'm the big sister."

Didi's mouth fell open. "Big sister?" She turned to Hannah. "Does this mean..."

Hannah bit her lip. "I have something for you." Sam's wife handed a small wrapped package to Didi.

"What's this?"

"Open it up and see."

Didi ripped the paper away. She turned to Luke and displayed the badge. "I'm going to be an honorary aunt. Can you pin this on my dress?"

Luke's hands were shaking as he freed the emblem from the cardboard holder and attached it to her dress. Didi turned to the older woman. "When are you due?"

Hannah laughed. "We just found out yesterday. I'll know more after our appointment with the obstetrician next week." Hannah reached for Sam's hand. "We decided to have a child now, and just started trying within the last month." She winked at Didi. "Guess we got it right on the first try."

TMI! Luke felt his face heat, but not as much as Sam's blush.

They sat down at the table. Hannah again turned her attention to Didi. "Were you limping when you walked in?"

Didi took Luke's hand in hers. "Um-hmm. I have news, too."

Hannah and Sam exchanged a puzzled look. "Which is?"

Didi took a deep breath. "I almost died. Luke saved me."

Sam pushed back from the table. "Saved you? What happened?"

Didi turned to Luke, but directed her words at the other couple. "We were at Bushkill Falls." She went on to describe her harrowing adventure.

The sparkle in her eyes as Didi spoke touched Luke. *Is that love?* His pulse was pounding.

Hannah wiped her eyes with a napkin. "I'm so glad he was there for you." She directed her gaze to Luke. "And you, sir, are a hero."

Didi squeezed his hand tighter. "Yep. My hero, but there's more."

Hannah's gaze returned to Didi. "More?"

Didi's full attention was on Luke. "Yes. Luke is more than my hero." Her smile was ear to ear. "He's my boyfriend."

Sam and Hannah exclaimed simultaneously, "Your boyfriend?" Hannah clapped her hands.

Luke had to blink twice to make sure this wasn't a dream. His words were soft. "Did I hear you right?"

Didi nodded and giggled. "Um-hmm. If that's okay..."

Luke quickly nodded. *I must be dreaming.* Didi touched his face and drew it close to hers. The girl's words were barely a whisper. "Yes. *My* boyfriend." Her lips found his and it was as if fireworks lit up the room. Her warmth, her taste... *Indescribably wonderful.* Without thinking, Luke's arms wrapped themselves around her as they explored each other's worlds. *This is Paradise.*

***

Hannah's joy was about to bubble over as she watched Didi and Luke kiss. She glanced over at Sam. His bright red face sported a scowl. He spit out his words. "Do you mind? My girls are watching."

Beth laughed. "You and Mom do this all the time."

Sam's head whipped toward his daughter. "That's different and I don't believe I asked for your opinion, young lady."

Hannah was floored and her anger rose. Beth's face paled and she looked down. *You've no right to talk to my daughter that way.* "Samuel. How dare you? Apologize to her, right this instant."

"Sorry, Beth." He turned to face the couple. "He saved you from... death?"

Didi grabbed a napkin from the table and blotted her lipstick from Luke's face. The young man stared at Didi with obvious wonder. "The only thing between me and the rocks below was fifty feet of air. Luckily, my foot got caught in a rope and Luke saved me."

Sam turned to Luke. "What? Did you shove her?"

Luke's face turned red and his fists clenched. "No! What kind of question is that?"

It suddenly dawned on Hannah. *Sam's jealous.* Why? "Sam, calm down." She turned to Didi. "Can you go over what happened, again?"

Hannah alternated glances between the couple and her husband. Sam's lips were clamped tightly together, but he followed the recap of their peril with obvious interest. Hannah reached for her husband's hand, but he quickly pulled from her grasp.

Their food arrived and Didi continued with the story of their week. When she mentioned that Luke had stayed in the hotel room with her each night because she was afraid, Sam left the table with the excuse of visiting the bathroom. He was calmer when he returned, but Hannah knew her husband well enough to know he was upset.

Later in the day, after the two couples had parted and the girls were busy, Hannah decided it was time to address the elephant in the room. "Didi was lucky Luke was there for her, wasn't she?"

Sam's hands clenched as he turned to Hannah. "I think there's more to the story."

She studied her man with curiosity. "Like what?"

"He had a duty to protect her, but there's something else. I'd like to know the *real* truth. She's not telling us everything."

Hannah touched his face. "I believe she did. What's going on?"

He turned away. "Nothing."

She gently turned his face to hers. "You can't lie to me, Samuel."

He gently pushed her hand away. "Don't call me Samuel."

She grasped his chin. "Okay, Sam. Are you jealous of Luke?"

"What? No."

Hannah assessed the man before her. "You still like Didi, don't you?"

Sam shook his head passionately. "She's the one who had a crush on me, not the other way around."

"I think she moved on." Sam glared at her. *It's so obvious why he's mad.* Her own anger intensified. "Remember, I'm the one you married. The one you proclaimed as your wife. The one carrying *your* child. Explain to me why you're so upset."

"He, he... he's not good enough for her."

"I see." She placed her index finger against her chin. "Who might be good enough to be with Didi?" She punched her finger against his chest. "If you're thinking it's you, tell me now."

Sam held his hands in front of him. "Hannah..."

She stepped closer, until they were almost nose to nose. "There's only one person in this world that I trust totally. And that's you. Don't give me a reason to change my mind, because if I do..." Hannah walked to the door. "If you give me a reason to think otherwise, I'll never trust you again."

Chapter 11

R iley's eyes slowly focused. The smoothness of the satin sheets and the comforting warmth and softness of the fleece blankets invited her to drift back to her dreams. The drive from the studio had seemed to drag on forever. Her dash clock read one fifty-five when she turned into the drive. But the giant of a man had been waiting on her. Mick had noted the exhaustion in her eyes and within ten minutes of her arrival, he'd tucked her in with a kiss before closing the door behind him. Just before he said goodnight, he whispered he had a surprise waiting for her in the morning.

She smiled, the lingering taste of his kiss still on her lips. *So this is what love feels like? Yes!*

A soft noise caught her attention. The sound was muffled, but she could readily identify it. Voices, specifically a young lady's voice. Riley's mouth was suddenly dry. *He has another woman in his house?* She'd ignored rumors about Mick's reputation as a playboy because he'd never given her a reason to doubt his faithfulness. *Told me he's in love with me.* If that was true, why was another woman in the house?

She quickly threw her robe around her shoulders and sneaked downstairs. The voices grew in volume. *Definitely a female's voice.*

The entrance to his kitchen was through a swinging door. Riley pushed it wide enough to see through the crack. A brunette with short, uncombed hair was standing behind Mick. The girl's hands were on his back, at the base of his neck, and she was massaging him. The unidentified woman wore a set of silky pajamas.

Riley's vision became bathed in red. She flung the door open hard enough that it slammed against the wall. The pair jumped and stared at her. "What in God's name is going on here?"

The woman's face broke into a wide smile. She strolled forward until she stood in front of Riley. "Is this the girl you told me about, Mikey?"

He turned and smiled, but his face was red. "Aye. Dis be Riley, and yes, she be da one I mentioned."

The stranger's eyes roved from head to toe. "Shapely... and prettier than you told me. Might even say she's beautiful."

He nodded. "Told ya so."

The woman reached for Riley's hand. "I think she'll be perfect."

An eerie feeling worked itself up her spine. *Perfect for what?* Riley pulled her hand away and retreated to the protection of the doorway. "Wh-what's going on and who are you?"

The woman laughed. "Thought he'd have told you about me. I'm Emma. Mikey's sister." Emma pulled Riley into a hug. "So glad to meet you. He asked me to come up this weekend so the two of us could get to know each other."

Now that everything was starting to make sense, Riley's vision returned to normal. "Nice to meet you, too." Riley shot Mick an angry look. "Would have been nice to give me a head's up. I was beginning to wonder when I heard another woman's voice downstairs."

Emma laughed louder, then turned to her brother and gently pinched his cheek. "Big oaf. You best be treatin' Miss Riley nice. You were miserable before you met her, so don't you dare be screwing this up." The sister pivoted and faced Riley. "I can guarantee you, Riley, there's no other woman in my brother's life. You see, he's in love with you."

Mick was suddenly there, wrapping his arms around Riley. "Emma, now be quiet. No need for my baby sister ta speak for me." Riley's chest tingled as he gazed into her eyes. "I love you, Riley Espenshade, purty heart and all." His lips softly touched hers and the room started to melt away.

Mick prepared a wonderful breakfast of chipped beef gravy and fried potatoes. While he cooked, Emma and Riley got to know each other. "Sorry for the confusion earlier. I wish Mickey would have told me his surprise was that I was going to meet his sister. He's talked about you quite a bit."

Emma's smile was comforting. "Yeah, well he's forgetful sometimes." She made a motion like she was smacking herself. "I think maybe he took one too many hockey sticks over his head, eh?"

Mick laughed as he cooked. "Maybe, but don't ya be thinkin' my hearin' ain't no good. We be in the same room, not?" The big man quickly delivered three heaping plates of food to the island in the kitchen. "I be hungry. Let's eat." He sat down and grabbed his fork.

Emma smacked his hand. "Where are your manners? You forgettin' to give thanks?"

Riley almost laughed as her man blushed. "Sorry." He reached for both women's hands. "Father, I be wantin' to say thanks for the bounty you gave us. For bringin' Riley into my life and for givin's me a wonderful sister. And I ask Ya to watch over Molly..." He stopped and drew a deep breath. "If it be in Your plans, please heal that li'l girl." He squeezed Riley's hand tightly. His lips were trembling. "And if'n it be possible, g-give that baby the family she be deservin'. Amen." He stood suddenly and grabbed Riley. "An' thank You again, for lettin' me find Riley. Ya know my dreams an' wishes, Lord. Please be makin' dem *all* come true. Amen."

***

Henry Campbell walked next to the police officer as they surveyed the damage to the field of young pine trees. "See how they're cut off on an angle? Like someone took a machete to them. This is the third act of vandalism in four months."

The officer shook his head. "I checked around. No one else has reported anything like this in Paradise or the surrounding communities. Anyone said anything to you?"

"No. Not a word."

"What do you estimate as the value of damages?"

Henry quickly did the calculation in his head. "Somewhere between ten to twenty thousand dollars."

"Hmm. Do you have any enemies or disgruntled employees... other than Kyle Parker?"

At the mention of the punk's name, Henry's anger flared. "Absolutely not. He's the only one I've fired and the single person who was the least bit difficult since I got here. I believe he's to blame."

The officer flipped through his notepad. "I checked into the dates the other incidents occurred. Mr. Parker was working and there were multiple witnesses who can..."

"You know as well as I do that Kyle Parker is behind this."

The officer stuffed his pad in his shirt pocket. "The evidence doesn't support that."

"It's plain as day to me. Perhaps I need to speak with him."

The officer sighed heavily. "Mr. Campbell, don't even consider trying to take matters into your own hands. Parker has a court order against you. Claims he fears for his life, because of how badly you beat him after the encounter with Sam Espenshade. This is a case for law enforcement. Let us do our jobs."

Henry forced himself to calm down. "I will, sir, but if he harms anyone in my family..."

The officer pointed his finger at Henry's face. "Don't even finish that sentence. I was glad when you dropped your charges last time, so I didn't have to arrest you. But don't think I won't throw the cuffs on if you cross the line. You understand me?"

Henry studied the man before answering, "Yes, sir."

The officer chewed his cheek as he considered Henry. "Good. I'll do some checking and if I discover anything, I'll let you know." The man's radio suddenly sprang to life and he answered it then said, "I've got to go. Motor vehicle accident. Take care, Mr. Campbell. I'll be in touch."

"Good day." Henry watched the man until he sped off in his cruiser. He turned in the direction of Christiana, where Kyle Parker lived. "You hurt my family, Kyle, and no piece of paper will save your soul from what I'll do to you."

***

Emma walked into the hospital, a few steps behind Riley and Mick. The scent of disinfectant was overwhelming. Her brother wanted her to meet the little girl he talked about. The big man also asked Emma to watch Riley's interactions with Molly.

They stopped at the nurse's station. One of the nurses smiled when they approached. "Mr. Campeau, good to see you again. Are you here to see Molly?"

Her brother stood tall. "Yea. And Mr. Campeau, that be my dad. You be callin' me Mickey, eh? How is she?"

The woman's smile turned into a frown. "She's having a bad day. Molly had a chemo treatment yesterday. Only time she quit crying was when you Skyped with her. She loves hearing your voice and looking at the photos you sent. Molly scrolls through the pictures constantly."

Emma noted Riley rubbing her brother's back. *Easy to see she loves him.* The nurse led them down the hall. Emma caught a glimpse of the bald-headed girl. She was on her side, staring out the window.

Mick said softly, "Molly?"

The baby turned and reached for him. Mick wrapped his arms around her, careful not to pull the tubes from her arms. Molly clung to him.

Emma was moved by the way he spoke softly, cradling the little girl like a china doll. "It's okay, Molly. Your Mickey's here." He changed his position so Riley could see the little girl.

Riley smiled. "Hi, Molly." She started tickling the girl's feet, but Molly pulled away and snuggled against Mick again.

Her brother motioned for Emma to come closer. "And dis is my sister, Emma. Can ya give her a smile?" Again, the child pulled closer to Mick.

Emma took a seat and watched Mick and Riley cuddle and talk with the patient. When Riley excused herself to find the restroom, Emma walked to her brother's side. "Have you told her yet?"

Her brother's expression turned troubled. "Don't think she be ready to hear it."

"I think it's gonna be hard enough on her, first you asking her to marry, then wanting to adopt Molly right away."

He nodded. "I know. Feels like I be cheatin' Riley." He turned to study his sister. "But my heart, it be tellin' me I gotta do dis."

Emma shook her head. "This little girl's going to require constant care. Expecting Riley to suddenly become a stay-at-home mom is probably not gonna go well."

"Aye, but Riley, she loves me, eh?"

The sound of a stretcher passing caught Emma's attention briefly. "That she does, Mikey, but I think you're asking too much."

He drew a deep breath. "Maybe. But what else could I do?"

Emma didn't have an answer. "Don't know, brother, but I think you need to ask the Big Man above for help."

He nodded. "I am, Emma. Every day, but He ain't give me a clue, yet."

Emma rubbed his shoulder. "He will. I just hope it's the answer you want."

Chapter 12

D idi closed her eyes and sent a silent prayer up to Heaven. *Please give me strength for this.*

Luke squeezed her hand and got her attention. "Don't worry, it'll be fine."

"Are you sure?"

He glanced her way. Those beautiful brown eyes seemed to twinkle. He nodded. "Never more sure of anything in my life." It seemed so apparent, but she wondered if what she was seeing was real.

But instead of being concerned about meeting Luke's parents, another thought pushed its way to the forefront. *Do you love me?* Didi prayed Luke felt the same as she did, but longed to hear him say it. "How do you know?"

He still held her hand, but was now concentrating on the road, apparently. "Because what's between you and me, it's special, Deeds. Nothing anyone ever says, or feels or anything else..." He drew a deep breath, then pulled his truck to the side of the road. He shifted the transmission lever into park and turned to her. His fingertips trembled as he touched her cheeks. "I need to say this. You're special, Deeds. Never in my life have I felt the way you make me feel. I'll confess I was attracted to you that first day, but..."

She couldn't help herself. She leaned forward and kissed him. The world no longer mattered. Luke's lips were warm and sweet as he pulled her close. Regretfully, she moved away. "I hope you know I feel the same way about you."

He pressed against her mouth again, then sat back. Luke's eyes gleamed. "I told you about Carter, how she broke my heart. Never thought I'd ever feel like this again, but... but something tells me you're not like her or any woman I've ever met. I want you to know I trust you with my whole heart." He lifted her hand and softly kissed it.

"I understand. You don't need to say it." *But I wish you would.* "Your actions at Bushkill spoke volumes."

Luke shook his head. "No, I want you to not just feel it, but also to hear it." His hands touched her head, just behind her ears and he drew her close enough she could feel his breath. "Deidre Susan Phillips, I... I'm in love with you, hopelessly and forever." Once again, he drew her to him. His lips found the mark as fireworks exploded in her mind.

Her hands caressed his hair and she pulled him against her. "I'm in love with you, too."

His smile was sweet as he touched her nose. "I prayed you did. Deeds, you're a dream. My dream come true."

He held her hand as they pulled back onto the state road and entered Columbia. The truck turned onto Route 441, then headed toward Millersville on Route 999. "My parents live here, in Washington Boro, the tomato capital of the state."

Didi drew a deep breath when Luke switched off the motor. Two flagpoles dominated the front yard. The taller flew the American flag, while the banner of the United States Marine Corps hung from the second.

Semper Fi.

She shivered slightly. Luke had warned her about his father, and how much of a bully the man could be. A thin woman with gray hair stepped out of the doorway and waved. Luke returned the gesture and made his way to the passenger door. Didi looked into his eyes and whispered, "I'm really nervous."

He wrapped his arms around her. "Don't be. Remember, to me you're perfect, so ignore him." He touched her nose. "We can't pick our parents, but we do get to choose who we spend our lives with." Luke kissed her softly. "Just remember not to judge me by my folks." He turned and led her to the lady. "Mom, this is my girlfriend, Didi Phillips."

Despite the smile, Didi knew the older woman was assessing her. "Nice to meet you, finally. My son's been talking about you for months. I was beginning to think I'd only see you on TV. Call me Angel."

"H-hello, Angel." Didi extended her hand, but the woman ignored it. Instead, she gave Didi a brief, but warm hug. The sound of someone clearing his throat commanded her attention. She glanced in the direction of the screen door.

The man's face was covered in salt and pepper whiskers that haphazardly reached his chest. His white tee-shirt was filthy. His head was bald, and dark brown eyes interrogated Didi's expression... or maybe it was her mere existence. "What, ain't I good enough to get introduced?"

Didi quickly shifted her gaze, catching the embarrassment in Luke's eyes.

"Sorry, Dad. This is Didi Phillips. Didi, my dad, Frank Zinn."

Frank didn't move, but continued to stare at Didi. "What happened to the doctor with the man's name?"

Luke's voice was shaky. "Carter and I broke up almost a year ago. But you knew that."

Frank nodded. "I remember. At least she wasn't blonde."

Didi's face heated. Angel hissed at him. "Frank! Show a little respect to Luke and his girlfriend."

The old man grunted and shoved the screen door open. "Might as well come in since you're here. Grub's about ready." His eyes ran up and down Didi's trim frame. "By the looks of things, you don't get enough to eat. Hope it's not because you don't know how to cook."

In respect to Luke, Didi ignored the insult. She entered the house, forced a smile and handed Frank the bottle of wine she'd brought. "This is a little 'pleased to meet you' gift."

He frowned as he examined it. "I drink Budweiser, not grape juice."

Why am I not surprised? "Sorry. Just trying to be kind."

He laughed. "Don't have to put any airs on around us. Have a seat at the table 'fore the food gets cold."

Luke held her chair for her, despite his father's obvious displeasure. Angel dished out the food—cabbage, potatoes, ham and homemade rolls.

Didi smiled. "Thank you. It smells delicious."

The older woman returned the gesture, but Luke's father answered, "It'll have to do. I'm sure a celebrity like you is used to fish eggs and champagne every night. Us working folk, we have to live within our means."

Luke was right. The old man's an obnoxious bully. "My parents are working class, too. They own a restaurant back home in Rapid City."

"Yeah? Then why aren't you home working for them?"

Didi drew a deep breath. "They encouraged me to reach for my dreams. I always wanted to be a newscaster."

The jerk emitted a demeaning laugh and stuffed his mouth with cabbage. Luke's hand found hers. Didi saw her boyfriend bow his head and followed suit. "We thank You, Lord, for this food and ask You to bless it and the maker of this wonderful meal. Amen." He squeezed Didi's hand extra tight.

The old man laughed again. "When'd you get religion, boy? Something they make you do in the Guard?"

Luke's fingers trembled. "Dad, can you at least be civil?"

His father seemed to ignore him. "Don't know why you couldn't go in the Corps like your brothers and sister." He turned to Didi. "I did thirty in the Marine Corps. Drill sergeant at Paris Island. His brothers turned out all right. Both in the infantry, but that weren't good enough for Lucas. He had to join the National Guard and become a sissy medic."

So annoying. A thought floated in, making things clear. Suddenly so obvious. *This man is the reason Carter broke off the engagement*. "Everyone has a different calling. I'm proud of Luke. Taking care of others when they're injured is a noble duty."

"Really? I think it's a coward's way of getting out of fighting. Not a job for a real man."

That's enough. Didi stood and faced the tyrant. Her hands were trembling. "I've known you what, not even half an hour? And you've insulted my intelligence, my cooking ability, my choice of a profession and the gift I brought. And do you know what? I don't care one bit what you think or say about me. If your tantrums are your way of trying to drive me off, think again. I *love* your son and I'm not going anywhere." Didi glanced around the table. Angel had her hand over her mouth, while Luke had his head buried in his hands.

Frank's face was red, hands on the table as if he were going to spring across it. "What could you *possibly* know about love, little girl?"

She ignored the bait. *This needs to be said*. "Go ahead, make your snide remarks about me, but how dare you insult Luke? In my eyes, he's a hero, and more of a man than you'll... than you'll ever be."

Frank stood, eyes glaring. "You ain't got no idea what it is to be a man, or a hero. A hero's someone who sacrifices himself for others with no regard for his own safety, something this boy would never do."

Didi leaned forward. "Really? It's a shame you don't know your son. He saved my life, did he tell you that?"

Frank took a step back. "Saved your life?"

Didi was so angry, saliva was on her lips. She stopped long enough to wipe her arm across her mouth. "Yes. At Bushkill Falls. I fell down the stairs and if my foot hadn't caught in a rope, I would have fallen to my death. And do you know what your *cowardly* son did?" Didi paused for effect, making sure the old man was watching her eyes. "Without a moment's hesitation, he leaped over the railing and saved me."

Luke's father shook his head. "Nice story."

Didi grabbed Luke's hand. "Did you stop to wonder about the stitches in his hand? From where they removed a five-inch sliver of wood when he grabbed the post trying to save my life. I don't care what you say, he's a great man, and by your own definition, a true hero."

Frank stared at his son. Angel looked as if she would cry. *I said too much.* Didi took a deep breath and addressed her boyfriend's mom. "I'm sorry for ruining the meal. It looks delicious, but I can't sit here and listen to him insult Luke." Didi's entire body trembled now. "If you'll excuse me, I need to get some air."

She hastened outside, finding a porch chair to sit on. *I let Luke down. Why didn't I keep my mouth shut?* But allowing anyone to talk about Luke that way... That was something she couldn't stomach. Didi jumped at the touch on her shoulder. She turned, expecting to find Luke, but instead, it was Frank.

The man nodded. "You got courage, girl. Standing up like that, I respect you. Sorry." He took a deep breath. "Guess I was wrong about my boy. Come on back in. Angel put a lot of effort into the meal and it'd be a shame to let it go to waste." A grin covered his face. "No offense, but eatin' a good home cooked meal might do you good. My wife made a special Dutch apple pie tonight. And besides, there's that bottle of wine you brought..."

Didi stood and faced him. "I didn't mean to be disrespectful in your home, Mr. Zinn. But please, don't insult your son like that again."

He nodded and studied her. "Luke never said anything about it. Another sign of a hero. My boy told me he got hurt at work, but never... Guess I misjudged him." He patted her shoulder. "Glad he was there for you. Why don't you come back inside and tell us all about it?"

Didi nodded. "Okay, Mr. Zinn."

He scratched his bare head. "And in the future, it's not Mr. Zinn. At least not to you. You gained my respect, Didi. *You* can call me Frank from now on."

Chapter 13

T he sharpness of the coffee contrasted with the homey scent of bacon. Riley stifled a yawn as Hannah poured her sister-in-law a second cup. "Since you work late, you don't have to come over so early."

Riley studied the other lady. Hannah had a glow about her even though she wasn't showing, yet. "Nonsense. I love spending time with you. It's just that Mickey and I were on the phone until three."

The gleam in Hannah's eye gave her away. *She's gonna tease me, again.* "And how is hockey's greatest superstar? And hottest lover?"

Riley's face heated. "Hannah, I'd never do that, at least not before marriage."

Hannah poured cream into her cup and took a sip. She didn't utter a word, but the teasing came through loud and clear when Hannah raised her eyebrows in a questioning manner.

"Now, wait a minute. You know me, and my values." *Best defense is a good offense.* Time to spar a little. "My brother was also raised that way, too, but I'm wondering if you corrupted him." She nodded toward Hannah's belly.

Hannah almost choked on her coffee as she laughed. "No, Sam was a gentleman. And he has your values. We waited."

Riley shot a questioning look. "Didn't wait very long after you two were married though, did he?"

Hannah shook her head before depositing more bacon and eggs on Riley's plate. *She knows I won't turn them down.* "Please, no more food."

"Tsk, tsk. Can't put 'em back, so you'll just have to eat up." Hannah refilled both cups. "Having children so soon was Sam's idea. We've agreed to have two babies. Your brother wants them now. How did he put it? Before their mother is too old?"

It was Riley's turn to chuckle. "That boy loves to tease you, doesn't he?"

Hannah nodded. "And I love it. He's the best friend I've ever known." The older lady let out a happy sigh. "Speaking of friends, have you talked to Didi lately?"

Riley swallowed her last strip of bacon and carried the empty plate to the sink before her sister-in-law could give her more. "Unfortunately, no. I used to see her a little in the afternoons, but these days she gets home after I leave." Riley eyed a sole piece of bacon still on the serving plate. It looked so lonely. "Mind if I finish it off? Just to put it out of its misery, you know?"

Hannah shook her head. "Please do. Didi and Luke seem to be spending every waking second together. Did I tell you he comes along to the bakery on Tuesday and Friday afternoons?"

"Really?" Riley hadn't known that. The last she'd heard was they were doing a series on fall activities in central Pennsylvania.

"He's quite nice. Told me he wants to learn to bake and asked if I minded." Riley caught the smile on Hannah's lips. "Luke said I'm the best baker he's ever met. I think they make a great couple. Same interests, same wacky sense of humor and they're so in love."

Riley suddenly missed Didi. Despite sharing an apartment in Lititz, they hadn't seen each other in weeks. "I knew she liked him, but I was worried. Workplace romances don't always work out."

Hannah giggled. "Sometimes they do. Look at Sam and me." Riley grew quiet. "How's it going with you and Mickey, really?"

Riley took a deep breath. "I don't know."

Hannah's expression changed. "I thought you two were in love?"

"We are, but..." Her voice trailed off.

Hannah reached for her hand. "But what?"

Riley's hand was trembling. "I-I don't know if I'm the right girl for him, that's all."

Hannah's eyes widened. "What? Why would you even say that?"

Riley took another sip of her coffee. "Because he wants things I'm just not ready for."

"Like what? What did he say?"

"It's not so much what he says, but his actions give him away. He's ready for marriage and... and a family. I'm not there, at all."

Hannah studied Riley's face. "It's only been six months since you met. Is there a rush for those things?"

"Not in my mind, but Hannah, when I see him with Molly and watch how he looks when he holds that little girl..." Riley shook her head. "I can sense he wants children, and now."

"Have you two discussed it?"

"No. And there's something else."

"As in?"

Riley stood and walked to the window. "As in, I'm not ready to give up my career."

"Who said you have to?"

Riley turned to her sister-in-law. "Another network contacted me about interviewing for a position. As a co-host."

Hannah shrugged. "So? New York's only a train ride away."

"It's not in New York. If I get the job, they'll want me to move to L.A."

***

Didi's heart was fluttering as Luke's truck stopped in front of the old farmhouse. His house. The one he bought last year and refinished. The place he talked about, with reverence and solitude. *He's sharing his dreams with me.*

The passenger door opened and he offered his hand. "Welcome to my humble abode. Let me give you the grand tour."

The exterior was immaculate. Blue shutters accented white vinyl siding. An oak door with stained glass side windows beckoned her to enter.

Gleaming wood rails and posts of the wrap-around porch were shiny, as if they had just been polished. Ceiling fans waited to be used and the grey floorboards were perfect. "It's beautiful. You did all this yourself?"

He nodded and Didi's heart filled with pride for this man. "There's still a lot to do." He pointed to the weed filled gardens along the porch. "I'd love to have a flower garden surrounding the foundation." He led her to an enclosed backyard. "I think a fountain with a fishpond would go great there. Maybe roses along the picket fence and a gazebo in the corner would complete the atmosphere."

She was impressed. "You have such great plans. What a wonderful home."

Luke's arms surrounded her as he pulled her back against his chest. "It's just a house right now. There's something missing that keeps it from being a home." *What's that?* He grew quiet and leaned his head against her. His lips touched her neck. "Want to see the inside?"

"Of course." He led her into the interior. The walls were ready to be painted, but the hardwood floors were breathtaking. "Are these original floors?"

A slight laugh escaped. "Heavens no. Simply plywood."

"Wow. It must have cost a fortune."

"Not if you do them yourself."

Didi turned to stare in marvel at this young man. "You did the floors, too?" He blushed a little as he nodded. "How'd you know how to do all this stuff?"

"Some of the guys in my unit work construction. They showed me the ropes."

You are something, Luke Bryan. "Unbelievable. I-I'm at a loss for words."

Luke grinned. "Well, that's a first."

"Smarty." Didi went on the attack, tickling his ribs.

He slowly pulled her in until they were face to face. "Deeds?" His expression changed to one of sincerity.

Didi was suddenly breathless. "Yes?"

His hands were shaking. He looked away momentarily. "I love you. Sorry there's not much furniture, but the kitchen is fully equipped. Want to keep me company while I make supper?"

That wasn't what you were going to say. What are you holding back? She decided to wait for Luke to continue later. "Only if I can help." His smile grew and a wonderful thought crossed her mind. "Hopefully this will be the first of many meals we'll make here, together." Luke only nodded, but she was pretty sure she could read his mind.

It felt so natural sharing the kitchen as they chopped veggies for a salad. Luke broiled salmon steaks. When the food was ready, he carried their plates into the massive living room. It had a beautiful gas fireplace, but the only other item was a large box. "I've been using this as a make-shift table. Hope that's okay."

"Um-hmm." *I wouldn't care if we ate at a dump, as long as we're together.* He lit the fireplace and retrieved two tall candles. Didi's heart fluttered again as they held hands to pray. His surprise was evident when she spoke. "Dear Father, we thank you for this food. I want to thank you for bringing this wonderful man into my life, not only to have saved me, but to share my life. Amen."

"Amen." His words were loud, because he pulled her into a deep and long hug. "How in the world did I get lucky enough to find you? This is paradise." His lips were wet and soft.

Didi held him close. "I'm the lucky one, winning your heart." The love in his eyes was so apparent.

After dinner, they washed the dishes and went back outside, despite the chill of the evening. Luke had a reclining yard chair. Didi climbed on his lap, her head snuggling against his shoulder as they watched the stars appear.

"I've always marveled at the stars. The light from some of them is hundreds, if not thousands of years old. We're looking at history here." A bright shooting star suddenly lit the night.

Luke's hands trembled as he held her. "I know, but the history we'll make is still before us. Deeds, I started to say something earlier, but stopped."

Didi sat up so she could see his eyes. *Please be what I hope for.* "I noticed. What were you going to say?"

His eyes gleamed. "Right now, this place is just a house. I hope someday to share it with the love of my life."

Me? Her heartbeat quickened. "And have you found her?"

His lips were soft. "I believe with all my heart I have. Will you help me turn this place into a home?

Let's make this into *our* dream home. In time, I mean."

Her eyes were suddenly blurry. She kissed him this time. "I'd love that, more than anything. Do you know how much I love you, Luke Bryan Zinn?"

A happy sigh left his lips as he pulled her close. "Yep. Just as much as I love you."

Chapter 14

K yle Parker crawled along the drainage ditch to get to his observation post. Most of the leaves had fallen, which eliminated his normal vegetation coverage. Arriving at the notch he had shoveled in the wall of the waterway, he raised the binoculars to catch a glimpse of the Campbell's operation without exposing too much of his head. His lips turned into a grin. *Right on time.* "Hello there, Edmund." Like clockwork, the youngest of the three brothers was conducting his evening tour to check the property. "I could set my watch by you, boy."

Kyle heard them coming. The whining of wheels approaching on the road forced his quick reaction. He fell to the bottom of the ditch, knowing he would be invisible to anyone passing by. Only the most observant would have noticed him, in his army surplus camouflaged fatigues.

He waited a full ninety seconds after the noise retreated before returning to his previous position. Edmund was nowhere in sight. "Where are you, you little limey?" His question was answered within seconds. Edmund walked into view from behind a clump of evergreen trees. The little man was picking up the empty soda cans Kyle had dropped from his drone last night.

In the distance, he watched as Edmund surveyed the area, looking for clues as to how the errant cans had appeared there. Edmund walked into the small copse of trees, right next to where he had his tool buried. *Atta boy. Right into where I'll set my trap.* The youngest Campbell searched for a few more moments before heading back to the office.

Kyle laughed to himself. His plans were set. Payback was coming. *Big time.* "Can't wait to see the look on your face when I get you." Kyle crawled off into the darkening evening.

***

Mick placed the call to Nashville and waited for Emma to pick up. Her smile was the first thing he saw as the live stream came on. "Hello, Mikey."

"How be my baby sister dis morning?"

"As good as a moose on a foggy morning. And you, brother, how's it going?"

"Well, my little one. Got somethin' to show you. Wanna see it?"

Her laughter drifted to him across the air waves. The same laugh she'd had all her life. *T'ank You for a wonderful li'l sis.* "Guess it depends on what you got to show me, eh?"

He reversed the camera and pointed it at the box. The brilliance of a diamond shone brightly in the kitchen light. "It be dis. For my Riley. Think she'll be likin' it?"

Emma let out a low whistle. "Holy cow, Mikey! How much did that set you back? Or did you steal the Hope diamond?"

He couldn't help but smile. "Didn't steal nothin'. Picked it up from da jewelers yesterday."

Her voice sobered. "Do you think she'll say yes? I mean, it's just a short time since you've been dating."

Mick shook his head. "Aye, you be right, but I think dis be true love, eh?"

Emma's sigh was loud enough to almost be felt. "Mikey, what's the plan if she says no?"

A slight involuntary shiver worked across his shoulder. "Ain't gonna happen. Riley, she be in love wid me. She tol' me so."

"I agree, but put yourself in her skates. Marrying you might not be too unbearable, but have you shared your thoughts with Riley about Molly yet?"

Mick pursed his lips and inhaled sharply. "Riley be a smart girl. She gotta know how I be feeling inside, eh?"

Emma was silent for a while. "Like I thought. You haven't told her yet. I think you best ponder on this for a while. And wait."

Mick rubbed his face, noting the sharpness of his whiskers. *Need to shave.* "I love dat girl."

"Yeah? Which one?"

He reversed the camera to see his sibling's face. "Riley, o' course."

Her eyebrows arched, like they always did when she didn't believe him. "More than Molly?"

"Listen, I be wantin' Riley as my bride."

She shook her head. "And still the great Mickey Campeau doesn't answer the question." Emma's lips turned into a frown. "I know what Riley means to you, but I'm worried *your* wishes might scare her off, eh?"

It was Mick's turn to frown. "Why'd I bother to call ya?"

"'Cause I'm your sister and I love you more than life itself." Her face softened. "Just worried your hurry might leave you with nothing, that's all. Sorry if the truth hurts, but I gotta be honest with you."

"T'anks, dream spoiler."

"Sticks an' stones may break these bones, but those words'll never hurt me, know why?"

He grunted. "No. Tell me."

"Because you love me, ya big lummox. Give Riley a hug for me."

"Yeah." She disconnected. Was Emma right? *Am I going too fast?*

***

Hannah held her youngest, Missi, on her lap. The three of them were waiting on Didi and Luke. Missi suddenly wriggled free and shot across the room. "Dee Bee!"

Didi dropped to her knees to catch the streaking child in her arms.

Hannah smiled as her youngest hugged not only Didi, but then reached for Luke. Hannah glanced at her husband, Sam. His eyes were crinkled as he took in the scene. *Thank You, God, for Sam.*

Hannah's mind went back to the conversation they'd had after the last time they dined with the other couple. She'd told Sam he better not give her a reason not to trust him. Then Hannah had walked out, slamming the door behind her. But before she'd taken even twenty steps or had a chance to wipe her cheeks, Sam touched her hand. *"Hannah, I need to tell you something."*

Hannah recalled the dread that filled her stomach. *"What?"*

"I need to tell you about last Christmas Eve, and what happened after I called you. Beth said you and your neighbor were back in your bedroom. Behind locked doors. I feared the worst."

She'd felt like her world was going to end. *"I thought we were past that."*

Sam had held her tightly. *"Didi and I, uh... we almost kissed."*

Hannah's mouth had been dry. *"Almost kissed?"*

"Yeah. I thought you and I were through, and Didi, she was right there. But my sisters intervened."

Hannah had been confused. *"Sisters?"*

"Riley walked in and broke it up."

Hannah had fought back the sob. *"Go on."*

"That night, Jenna came to me in a dream. She reminded me why you were here, and, and what you meant to me." Before she could question, he had continued. *"Jenna told me that you were my destiny, my future."* Sam had stopped so she could digest his words. *"My true love. I will never, ever, allow anything to come between us. You are my world, not just my wife. My soulmate and best friend. I love you and only you, Hannah Espenshade, forever."*

Hannah had read his heart and truly believed him. The memory of that next kiss was simply amazing, even after all this time.

Didi and Luke stood before them now, Missi snuggling in Luke's arms. The young blonde looked so happy. "This was a great suggestion before we head over to Sight and Sound Theatre. We've never eaten at Hershey Farms. Does the food taste as great as it smells?"

Sam spoke before Hannah could. He tightly squeezed her hand. "Yep. Early in our courtship, I brought Hannah and the girls here. I was trying to impress her, you know?" He held his hand to the side of his mouth, as if to tell a secret. "I think it worked."

Hannah reached over and kissed his chin. "Your actions are what drew me to you, not where we ate." She turned to the couple. "You two going to sit down?"

Luke carried Missi to her chair. "Here you go, *Cindy*."

The five year old placed her hands on her hips. "I'm not Cinderella anymore. I'm Moana. And I want Dee Bee to sit next to me."

All four adults laughed. They ordered their soft drinks and visited the smorgasbord offering. Sam turned to Missi. "Can you say the prayer?"

"No, Daddy. You do it." Hannah's eyes were moist. Only in the last week had Missi started calling Sam 'daddy'.

"Okay, Moana. Father, we thank You for this food and for the friends sharing the table tonight. Let the food nourish our bodies." He again gave

Hannah's hand a tight grip. "Lord, please bless Didi and Luke with happiness, just like you've given us."

Hannah noted the kiss Luke and Didi shared. Didi took a deep breath before speaking. "Have some news." Everyone got quiet. "Oh, by the way, where's Beth?"

"She's at her friend Selena's, for a sleepover." Hannah was impatiently excited. "What's the news?"

Didi and Luke smiled at each other. "Luke's coming home with me at Christmas. He wants to meet my parents."

Sam and Hannah shared a look of surprise. "So soon? What do your parents think of that?"

Didi's smile was ear to ear. "They can't wait."

Luke turned and spilled his soda on Didi. "Oh sweetheart, I'm sorry."

The girl laughed and excused herself so she could clean off her dress. When she was out of earshot, Luke spoke. "Forgive me. That was intentional. I wanted to tell you something and I, uh, I want it to be a surprise for Deeds." He waited until they were both looking at him. "You're our best friends." He turned to look directly at Hannah. "I know she thinks of you as a sister, Hannah. I'm going to ask her parents for permission to propose to her."

Hannah had to hold back her shriek of delight. "I am so excited! You think Didi will say yes?"

He hurried his response as Didi worked her way back to the table. "Without a doubt. You should know how much I love and cherish her. Now remember, it's a surprise." Luke stood and held Didi's chair. "I apologize again, Deeds."

The girl looked around the table with questioning eyes. "What happened? Did I miss something?"

Luke was quick in his response. "No. We were just talking about the charity ball at the tea room. You know, the one on Christmas Eve? Hannah and Sam are going to share a table with us." He quickly winked at Hannah and her hubby.

Sam, the sly little devil, quipped, "Yeah. Luke and I were discussing which songs we want to request."

Didi's look was one of doubt as she studied Sam. "And what song will you request for the two of you?"

"*Unchained Melody*. You know, by the Righteous Brothers."

Didi didn't remove her gaze from Sam's eyes. "And which one did Luke pick out?"

Hannah saw her husband's deer-in-the-headlight look. She also captured Luke's mouthed reply. Sam squinted as he tried to read Luke's lips without Didi noticing. "That's, uh, easy. Lazier, by, uh, Taylor Swit, I mean Swift?"

Didi stood, hands on her hips as she alternated her gaze between Sam and Luke. "I'm lazy? Is that what you think?"

Hannah tried to keep it in, but a loud giggle erupted from her lips. Hannah knew her friend well enough to see Didi was teasing them. "I'm waiting for an answer." She turned to her boyfriend. "Lazier? Really? And this coming from *you*?"

Luke's face was red. "Deeds, no. I said *Crazier*, not lazier."

Sam piped up. "Isn't that what I said? Oh, maybe I mispronounced it."

Good recovery. Didi didn't even turn to look at Sam. Instead, she walked closer to Luke. "So now I'm crazy? Huh." Didi crossed her arms and shot him a stern look, but Hannah could see the smile tugging at the corner of her lips. "And all this time, I thought you liked me. I can't believe my ears. The man I love says I'm a nut case."

Luke gently touched her arms, his expression sincere. "No. The song is *Crazier* by Tay-Tay. It reminds me of you, especially where she sings, 'You lift my feet off the ground, spin me around... make me feel crazier, crazier'."

Hannah could tell there was no way Didi was going to let Luke off the hook. "Sure it's not the line, 'I was trying to fly, but I didn't have wings'? I think you're making fun of me, when I almost fell to my death on the stairs when you were being bullheaded."

The color left Luke's face. "No, Deeds. Swear I wasn't making fun of you."

Didi poked him in the chest. "You guys weren't talking about songs, were you?"

Hannah knew Luke well enough to know he wouldn't lie. *Not to his 'Deeds'.* He slowly shook his head. "Can't keep anything from you. I was telling Hannah and Sam..."

Didi quickly kissed him. "Be quiet. I'll wait until you're ready to tell me." Hannah could see the puzzlement in Luke's eyes. "I'll never force you to do or say anything. I trust and love you, Lucas Bryan." She took his hands. "Even if you are a goofball."

Hannah couldn't help it. Laughter spilled out. But Didi and Luke didn't notice. Luke touched her cheek. "Maybe, but I'm *your* goofball."

Didi kissed his lips again. "And I love it."

Chapter 15

R iley grabbed her carry-on from the overhead compartment. The interview had gone better than she dreamed possible. They'd offered her the job, right on the spot. If she accepted, Riley would be *the* lead anchor for the sports center the new network was launching.

A voice in her head nagged at her conscience. *But I'd have to live on the west coast, so far from my family and Mickey.* Her relationship with the hockey star was strong, but still, this might be difficult. *He travels all the time, so would the distance actually be a problem?*

She was contemplating that question as she exited the security checkpoint. "Hey, sis. Have a good flight?" So deep in thought, Riley almost walked past her brother.

"Not too bad. This is nice, you being my ride to and from the airport."

Sam laughed and his crooked smile shone back at her. "Don't mind at all. Sorry about your car."

Just as she was getting ready to leave for the airport, her car's engine had coughed, then died. When she tried to restart the vehicle, a terrible grinding noise came from under the hood. She'd called Hannah and within twenty minutes, Sam arrived. "The garage called. Something about slipped motor bearings. Luckily, it's under warranty."

"Good thing." He took her luggage.

"I'll carry that. You've got your bad leg and cane. Let me do it."

"Nope." They walked outside to catch a shuttle to hourly parking. "So why'd you go to L.A.?"

"Business."

He turned and watched her eyes. "Out there for a game? I didn't see you on TV."

Forgot he watches the news, just for me. Sam was such a great brother. As a kid, he'd been so close to Jenna, their other sister. The one who died. *Miss you, Jenna.* Within the last year, Sam and Riley had drawn closer. Riley realized she had taken Jenna's place in his heart.

He cleared his throat. "You hear my question, or was it too noisy?"

Time to come clean. "I had a job interview."

Sam's face turned white. "What? You just moved back from Cleveland this summer."

Riley had to look down. Her fingers were fidgety. "You remember when you were chasing your dream of playing pro baseball?" When her brother didn't respond, she looked at him. He nodded. "This is my dream."

"But the west coast is three thousand miles away."

"Please don't make this harder on me. I was hoping you, of all people, would understand and support me."

Sam wiped his face with his hand and pinched his nose. "Of course I will. It's just, well, I kind of got used to you living here. Missed you so much when you were in Cleveland. And my girls idolize you. They love having their aunt close by."

"Sam..."

"Okay. No more guilt trips. Have you told Mickey?"

I dread telling him. "No, not yet."

"What do you think he'll say?"

With more conviction than she felt, she replied, "I'm sure he'll understand. He travels to all those away games."

They disembarked the shuttle and headed to the elevator. "When are you going to tell him?"

"At the charity ball, Christmas Eve."

***

Henry Campbell pushed his chair back from the monitor, almost running over Edmund's foot. Edmund shook his head. "I don't understand how this trash just appears there."

"Me neither. It's like it falls out of the sky. Replay that segment again."

Henry returned to the monitor and rewound the digital image. Edmund was leaning right against him.

"See what I mean? The bag just appears to float down, out of the sky. Could it be the wind?"

Henry reviewed it again. His chin rested against the palm of his hand. He could feel Edmund's breath against his ear and caught a whiff of black licorice. Edmund was addicted to Twizzlers. "Somehow, I don't think so. Let's get another camera out there, but point this one up higher. Let's see if we can solve this mystery."

Henry watched as Edmund stood. *I'm thankful for you, brother.* For many years Edmund had been distant, but since his wedding to Tara, he'd turned around. Edmund now managed many things around the farm, allowing Henry to spend more time with his family. "I'll order it tonight. With the holiday, we might not get it delivered until after Christmas."

"That's fine. Hey, did you and Tara find someone to watch your daughter? Wait. You two *are* coming to the ball tomorrow, right?"

Edmund nodded. "Yep. Tara's mum's gonna watch her. Who's gonna watch your girls?"

Henry laughed. "Tara's mum. Guess the cousins will have extra play time together."

Edmund touched Henry's arm. "Thank you, Henry."

Thank you? "For what?"

Edmund chewed his lip momentarily. "For forgiving my sins. My life would be so much less if we didn't have such a close family."

Scenes from years of adversity with Edmund crossed Henry's mind. And now? Edmund had never been closer to everyone in the family as he was lately. "I'm proud to have you as my brother." They shook hands, their grip lingering. "I'm looking forward to the ball. I know the girls have been shopping for dresses, and don't forget the accessories."

Edmund laughed. "Yeah. Should have seen the hit to the checkbook from Tara's shopping spree.

Told her she might have to increase her hours at the office to pay for all of it." The younger man stretched. "Well, I need to get home. My girls are waiting."

Henry nodded. "Mine, too. 'Night, brother."

"G'night." Edmund departed.

Henry sat down and watched the video stream again. He hadn't shared it with Edmund, but Henry was pretty sure he knew how the debris found its way to their property. In the Special Boat Service of Her Majesty, his strike team had dropped listening devices into the terrorist's camps using the same stealth technology. *So you got yourself a drone, huh Kyle?* The new camera would tell him if his suspicions were correct. If Henry was right, he and Kyle would have a long talk. The villain's face appeared before his eyes. "If I'm right, you can be damn sure it won't be pleasant for you."

***

Didi slid off the seat of her Escape, reaching for the hand of her dream, her Luke. He leaned down and kissed her. "In all my years, I've never seen a more wonderful sight. You look beautiful tonight, Deeds."

Heat rose in her cheeks. *You're absolutely wonderful, Luke.* "Wasn't sure if my dress would be good enough, seeing how you're decked out in a tux, Mr. Bryan."

Luke held her head. "Hey, before we go in, I wanted to thank you again for last night. You know, everyone loved you."

Didi closed her eyes and visions of the previous evening filled her head. Luke's unit held their annual Christmas party. And everyone had treated her like a celebrity. "Such a nice group of people. I'm not wild about you being in the service, but the guys in your unit are a great bunch. Almost like you're a band of brothers."

"And sisters. Remember there are five women in our unit."

Didi nodded. He had introduced her to everyone. *As the love of his life!* "What a wonderful couple of days. Last evening, the ball tonight, and then the two of us flying home to see my parents tomorrow. They're gonna love you."

He kissed her again. "I hope so. If your mom and dad don't, they'll have to get used to me because I plan on hanging around with you, for like... forever."

The exhilaration of just being with Luke was breathtaking. She took his arm as they entered the building. Sophie Miller, owner of the tea room, greeted them with a smile. Didi loved her British accent. "Merry Christmas, you two. Welcome to Essence of Tuscany and thank you for supporting the cancer fundraiser tonight. May I help you find seats?"

Before Didi could answer, Hannah was there. She gave both Didi and Luke a quick hug. "Didi, don't you look dazzling tonight? I think pink is your color." She turned to Luke. "And here's Luke Bryan. Wow, you really clean up well."

Sophie patted him on the shoulder. "Ignore her. I think you look absolutely dashing, Luke."

Hannah winked at Didi. "We saved you seats." She pointed to a table. Sam grinned and waved. "After you get your food, come sit with us."

Luke held Didi's hand as they strolled to the bounty-filled serving trays. Within seconds, their plates were laden with shrimp, crab balls, cheese, veggies and Swedish meatballs. Luke touched her arm and pointed at the pastries. "Look. There's the swans and gingerbread men we helped Hannah make."

"They look tasty, don't they?"

Luke lifted her chin and softly touched her lips. "Nothing could be sweeter than your kisses."

Didi was almost overcome with joy. The pretty blonde set her plate on the table and wrapped him in her arms. "Don't know what I did to deserve it, but I have to tell you something. You're the best thing to ever happen to me."

There was a twinkle in his eyes. "Deeds, do you really, and I mean in your heart, really know how I feel about you?"

Yes, yes! However, she couldn't resist teasing him. "I think you might like me, a little."

He laughed. "No. I like you more than anyone I've ever met, and then there's this other thing..."

It was her turn to giggle. "Which is?"

He framed her face in his hands. "I'm in love with you."

Their lips blended together. *Never dreamed love could be so wonderful.*

A gruff voice interrupted them. "Hey now. Don't ya be pickin' on my friend Didi, eh? If'n ya are, we be takin' this outside."

Luke tensed in her embrace.

Didi turned to find Mick and Riley standing there, holding hands. Despite his gruff voice, the hockey star sported a smile. He wrinkled his nose as he addressed Didi. "He be botherin' you, ma'am? I can handle him, if'n you want. He be pretty small... an' puny."

Riley laughed and joined the banter. "I think it's consensual. Maybe you two need to get a room." Riley hugged Didi, and then offered her hand to Luke. "Nice to see you again. This is my boyfriend, Mickey Campeau. Ignore his words. Despite being a tough hockey player, he's actually a nice guy once you get to know him." Riley paused for effect as she turned to her man. "Eh?"

Mick ripped Riley off the floor as he hugged her and twirled her around. "Don't be tellin' my secrets outta school now, okay? I only saves dis side of me for you." Didi caught the merriment in his voice as he teased Riley. "Eh?"

After they'd all filled their plates, Didi led them back to the Espenshade table. The meal was so much fun, though not a single person was exempt from the good natured teasing. Didi did notice Riley seemed to be exceptionally quiet. *What's that about?* After dinner, a lady from the American Cancer Society gave a short speech and thanked everyone for their support. When she was finished, the DJ took over. Luke excused himself from the table. The next song happened to be *Unchained Melody*. Didi saw Sam struggle to his feet and offer his hand to Hannah.

Someone clearing his throat caught her attention. She turned to find Luke, bowing before her. "Deeds, would you allow me the honor of dancing with the prettiest girl in the world?"

Not so fast, Mr. Bryan. Didi pretended to be offended. "What? You want to dance with Riley?"

His smile made her tremble. "No, silly. We need to get your hearing checked. Let me rephrase. I meant the most beautiful girl in the entire universe. And to me, that is you, Deidre."

Tonight's so magical. Luke held her tightly as they danced. They fit together perfectly. *Like we're made for each other.* "I love you, Luke."

After that song, the opening strains to *Crazier* filled the air. Luke kissed her ear as he held her. "Listen to the words, Deeds. This is truly how I feel, when we're together." Luke's deep voice sang along with Taylor Swift. "You lift my feet off the ground, spin me around... you make me crazier, crazier..."

Didi's head rested on his shoulder. *Can my life get happier than this?*

***

Riley watched the other two couples dance. Dread filled her mind. Tonight was such a romantic evening, well for other people, but not for her. *I need to tell Mickey the truth.* What would he say?

The big man was quiet now, watching her. "Everything be alright wid you?"

Riley forced a smile. "Just have a lot on my mind, that's all."

His hand softly covered hers. "Ain't good at it, but would you be wantin' to dance?"

I'm going to miss you. "Mind if we just sit here together?"

"You be sad. Got just the ting to brighten you up. Ya game?"

The love in his eyes was so apparent. *So much harder than I thought.* "That would be nice."

He took a deep breath and shot her a warm smile. Then he stood up and turned toward the DJ. "Hey you! Turn off da music for a minute." He placed his right hand in his pocket. "Can I get everyone's attention?"

Riley felt her face heat. *What in the world?* She hissed, "Mick, stop it. Everyone's looking at you."

He turned and winked before pivoting and sweeping his arm, as if to draw even more attention. "Sam, Hannah, Didi and uh, what's his name. Come over here."

Riley felt as if her entire body was on fire from embarrassment. Her mouth was open as the other two couples arrived. Mick suddenly dropped to one knee. She caught a glimpse of a small red box in his right hand. *No, please, no.* Before she could speak, Mick grasped her right hand with his left.

"Riley Espenshade, findin' you was the best thing ever for me. Don't know if you're aware, but I be in love wid you dat first day, you know, at Ashley's wedding. You is so purty, not just yer face, but inside, in yer heart." He popped open the box to display the largest diamond she'd ever seen, set on a beautifully engraved white gold band. "Riley, I'm wantin' you to marry me, to be my wife. Will you marry me?"

Please God. Not now! She chanced a quick look at her brother and sister-in-law. They were waiting for her to respond. Hannah was all smiles, but Sam's expression was sober as he watched the scene. Her view shifted to Luke and Didi. They were holding each other, watching in apparent wistful glee. She shifted to Mick's face. His joy was so apparent. *I can't. Need to tell him.*

But to turn him down now would publicly humiliate him. She had no choice. Riley nodded and the answer seemed to come from someone else. "Yes."

Chapter 16

M ick kissed her lips and slipped the ring on her finger. "Thank you, Riley. I be da happiest man in da world." The DJ played a romantic song. Mick lifted her up and led her to the center of the now deserted dance floor. "You 'n' me, we should talk about a weddin' date. How's 'bout New Year's Eve?" Never before had he felt this happy. *Wish Emma woulda been here.*

Riley's chin was trembling. "I-I-I, uh, think we should just let this sink in first."

He couldn't help but laugh. "Nope. Ain't takin' da chance a' you changin' yer mind. I love you so much, an' thinkin' a' bein' yer husband, it be makin' me tingle inside." His dreams were coming true. *Time to tell Riley* all *my thoughts.* "An' after the honeymoon, we can set up house and start a family. Whatcha think about adoptin' Molly?"

Riley stopped dancing and pulled away. "C-can we go outside and talk?"

The strange sensation gripping his shoulders made him shiver. "Why can't we talk here?"

She grasped both his hands. "Please, Mickey? I need some air."

Somethin's wrong. "If'n you want to, okay."

She led him outside, to a night blanketed under millions of stars. The tangy scent of a wood fire filled the air. Riley stood with her back toward him. "I do somethin' wrong?"

When she turned, he could see the lines of moisture from her eyes. "I wish you would have waited, and... and not proposed in someplace so public. Or at least given me some indication of what you were planning. I mean, that was a big shock, but then you want an instant family, too? Don't you think you could have asked my opinion first?"

She does love me, don't she? "Den go ahead. Talk to me 'n tell me yer thoughts. I be your fiancé, yer best friend, so go ahead."

He'd never seen the look that now covered her face. A chill gripped his spine. Riley was looking everywhere but at him. "I, uh, need to tell you something."

Another couple walked outside and stood close by. Riley grabbed his hand and yanked him away.

"Riley, you be scarin' me."

She rubbed her arm across her eyes and let out a sob. "Mickey, I took a job in Los Angeles. Another network offered me a new position, to anchor the new sports network they're launching."

What? His hair seemed to be standing on end. "A' course, you told 'em no, eh?"

Riley was struggling to keep from crying. "No. I accepted."

His breath came out in short bursts, the moisture vaporizing in the cold night air. "But I jus' asked you to be my wife. An' you said yep."

126

Riley curled her right fist and slammed it against her leg. Her face was filled with anger. "What choice did I have? To tell you no in front of everyone would have embarrassed you to no end. And then, and then, you dropped it on me that you want to adopt Molly and set up house?" She took a deep breath and touched his cheeks. "I'd love nothing more than to be your wife, but... but I have dreams, too. This job is what I've always wanted. What I've worked for. And those dreams are right before me..."

"I'm right before you, too." Disappointment nagged at his mind. "An' in your mind, you got a decision ta make, right? Or'd ya already make it?"

She shook her head. "You don't understand how hard this is. I need time, to think... to decide where we fit in."

His hands twitched in anger. "No, you need to decide if'n I be fittin' into yer plans at all, eh?"

Riley's head was tilted. He followed the path of one of the tears that fell from her cheek to the ground below. "I said yes, but I need some time to think, to know what to do."

He was having trouble stopping the feelings building up inside of him. Mick stepped away from her. "I can see it in yer face. You *don't* want to be my wife, do ya?"

"I do, I do, just... just not right now." He watched in disbelief as she slipped the ring from her finger and offered it back to him. "Let's wait a little, okay?"

His anger exploded and everything turned red. "I can't wait. Neither can Molly. I want a final answer 'n I be wantin' it right now!"

Riley was sobbing. "I can't give you one. I need time to think."

The pain in his chest was the worst he'd ever felt. *I be such a fool.* He grabbed the ring from her and threw it as hard as he could into the darkness. "No different den the others. Goodbye and good riddance, Riley Espenshade." Mick turned and stumbled off into the night.

***

Didi was laughing so hard, she had trouble staying on her chair. Luke and Sam were discussing pranks they were going to pull at Riley's wedding. Luke pointed at Sam. "Beat this one. We'll plant a cell phone in the choir loft. Then call it when Riley's walking down the aisle."

Sam held his stomach as he laughed. "And for a ring tone, let's make it *Help* by the Beatles."

Hannah was snickering in her eggnog. Didi curbed her laughter when Hannah lightly touched her arm and nodded in the direction of the door. Turning, Didi couldn't believe her eyes. Riley had both hands covering her mouth as she stumbled in from the outside. Didi immediately headed to her friend, with Hannah a half step behind.

Sam's sister was crying when Didi reached her. "Riley, what's wrong?"

Riley couldn't stop sobbing. "He, he... Mickey broke it off..."

The tea room was becoming silent. *Need to get her away from prying eyes.* "How about if Hannah and I take you to the ladies room?"

Riley nodded.

Sam was suddenly there. Didi caught the look of concern on his face. "Sis, what's going on? I thought you said yes."

Riley could only shake her head. Hannah touched his hand. "I'll take care of her. Just hang out for a few minutes."

Sam reached for Riley's hand. She pulled him in, clinging as if he were her life preserver. A man Didi didn't recognize was there suddenly, holding a phone in front of him. Sam turned his back so the man's view of Riley was blocked.

Hannah was more proactive. She confronted the man. "Do you mind? This is a private issue."

The stranger tried to slip past, still pointing his phone toward Sam and Riley. He laughed at Hannah. "Isn't that the girl Mickey Campeau just proposed to? Why's she crying? Did she and Mickey..."

The man's words stopped suddenly. Didi had been looking at Riley, but her curiosity got the better of her. She spun around. Luke had the man's camera hand clamped between his fingers.

The guy tried to push Luke away. "Stop it. You're hurting me."

Luke ripped the phone away and shoved him rudely before doing something to the phone.

"Give me my phone back!"

Luke threw the device at him. "Get away from my friends." The man glared at Luke and looked him up and down, as if assessing him.

Before the man could move, Sophie appeared with a familiar face right behind her. The hostess addressed the rude man. "Sir, I think it would be best for you to leave. This instant."

He stuck his finger in Sophie's face. "You can't tell me when to go."

In disbelief, Didi watched as the redheaded man who had accompanied Sophie grabbed the jerk's arm and twisted it violently. The man with the phone dropped to his knees as the redheaded gentleman continued to yank the man's arm even more. In a deep voice with a Scottish accent, he whispered harshly, "How dare you point your finger at Sophie? She's my best friend and *deserves* respect. And you better learn that lesson, immediately."

"Quit that. It hurts! Who are you?"

"Henry Campbell. You want to leave peacefully or should I provide you with some assistance?"

"Okay, okay. I'll go, but I want my money back."

Henry released the man's arm and shoved him on the floor. Henry removed his wallet and threw some bills in the man's face. "You got what you wanted. You have three seconds to leave." The man scooped the money from the floor and started to walk away. Then he stopped and opened his mouth, but didn't finish his sentence. That was because Henry Campbell rapidly strode toward him.

Sophie spoke softly. "Let's move this into the kitchen." Didi caught Sam's nod as he led Riley away. Sophie held the swinging door open for them. "You'll have some privacy in there. Henry and I will guarantee it."

Didi followed Hannah into the kitchen, right behind Sam and Riley. Didi jumped at the touch against her arm. Luke had followed and grasped her hand tightly.

Everyone waited until Riley calmed down. Her friend wiped her eyes. "Great. I'm sure everyone will see that on the internet."

Luke patted Riley's shoulder. "No, they won't. I deleted his video before I handed the phone back."

Riley nodded and touched his hand. "Thank you."

Luke reassured, "That's what friends are for."

Hannah held Riley's free hand. "What happened?"

Riley wiped her arm across her face. "Mickey, he... he broke up with me."

Hannah smoothed her hair. "Why? He just proposed? Maybe this is all a big misunderstanding."

Riley shook her head. "No. When I handed the ring back, he threw it away and said 'good riddance'. Can someone give me a ride home?"

Her brother's words were quiet. "This is all because you took the job in L.A."

His sister sobbed hard. "Yes."

Job in L.A.? Didi spoke before she thought. "What are you talking about?"

"I accepted a job as a news anchor in Los Angeles."

Didi looked at Hannah. Hannah closed her eyes, then shook her head. "The job on the west coast you told me about?" Riley nodded. "When do you have to leave?"

Riley sniffled, hard. "Tomorrow."

Chapter 17

Luke couldn't get his hands to stop shaking. Didi slid the rental to the curb in front of a beautifully decorated Cape Cod. The street was lined with vehicles. Garland was strung along the rails of the porch. Red, silver and gold balls hung on the twin white pines bracketing the walk. He jumped when her warm hand touched his. That pretty smile greeted him as he turned toward Didi. "You're trembling, Luke. It'll be fine. My parents are two of the nicest people I've ever met... and they'll love you."

"Hope so. Guess I know how you felt when you met my folks." Didi leaned across and kissed him. The homey scent of pines awaited as he opened his door and walked around the vehicle to help Didi out. *Please let them like me. And let them say 'yes'.*

Before Didi was completely out of the car, the front door opened and a couple stepped onto the porch. Although older than Didi, the woman's face resembled her daughter. She ran with open arms to hug Didi. The man approached with such an engaging smile, it helped wash away Luke's nervousness. Her father waited for his turn to hug his daughter.

"My baby. Missed you so much." The man kissed Didi on the cheek, then slid an arm around her waist. He nodded at Luke. "Is this the young man you told us about?"

Didi's smile had never been as wide. "It sure is. The one and only Luke Bryan Zinn."

The merriment in the man's eyes was contagious. "Pleased to meet you." He reached for Luke's hand and gripped it warmly. "You sing like the real Luke Bryan?"

The warmth that filled Luke's cheeks flowed into his arms. "No sir, uh, the whole Luke Bryan thing was a... a joke I tried to play on your daughter."

Her father laughed. "She told us. How about I give you a hand with the luggage? My name's Phil, by the way, and this is my wife, Brenda."

Luke turned to Didi's mom and was met with a tight hug. "Luke, we've heard so much about you." She held his face in both hands, her voice cracking as she whispered, "Didi told us how you s-s-saved her life. Th-thank you."

Luke and Phil carried the luggage into the house. The pleasant essence of cinnamon and baked ham filled the home. Quite a few other people were waiting inside. Didi turned to Luke. "Let me introduce you to *our* family." Those beautiful blue eyes were full of merriment. "Pay close attention. There will be a quiz afterwards." An assembly of aunts, uncles, cousins and children waited in line. Each hugged Didi and greeted Luke warmly.

The inside of the home was meticulously decorated. When everyone walked into the next room, Luke struggled to keep his mouth from hanging open as he took in the photos hanging on the walls. Pictures of Didi lined almost every square inch—photos of her as a baby, then a child, finally as a teenager, every stage of growing up.

Laughter from the kitchen drew his attention. *Didi's laugh, so beautiful.* Happiness and love seemed to fill every inch of this wonderful place. *So different than where I grew up.* A soft touch on his arm caught his attention.

Brenda's smile warmed him. "As you can see, our daughter means the world to us. The greatest blessing of our life." She lifted a baby photo from the wall, her fingers softly stroking the image in the frame. "We tried for fifteen years to have a child, but I could never get pregnant. Finally, we gave up hope. Six months later, I started getting ill every morning. Imagine our shock, and joy, when the doctor told us I was carrying a child. I was thirty-seven." Brenda took a deep breath and her eyes grew large for a brief second. When she turned to face him, her cheeks were moist. "She told me how close she was to falling to her death... about how you jumped over that railing to save her life. I couldn't have gone on if she, if she... I love her so much."

Luke opened his arms and Brenda hugged him, tightly. "I know exactly how you feel. Didi's my entire world, and I love her, too."

Brenda squeezed him tightly. "I know."

"Ahem." Luke turned to find Phil eyeing him strangely. "Isn't this peculiar? You come to our home, arm around my daughter, and now what do I find? You're making a move on my wife."

***

Mick watched little Molly as she slept. His voice was faint. "Looks like it just be you an' me, li'l one." Her eyes winced as she repositioned herself. "All my dreams, of you an' me an' Riley bein' a family... Guess dey be gone, eh?" *Can't believe she took da job over me.* In his mind, he could see the three of them together, Molly between them, her little fists holding onto their fingers as they walked on a trail along a lake.

"Mr. Campeau?" The nurse's words brought him back to the here and now.

"Yep?"

He turned to find a nurse named Tammy standing there. She always seemed to be at the hospital. "Good morning. Can I get you anything?"

"No. Can't stay. Game dis afternoon. Just wanted to see my li'l Molly, dat's all." Mick took note of the strange look in her eye. "Everythin' be alright, eh?"

Tammy's face seemed to darken. "Did anyone mention to you what's going on with Molly?"

The woman's expression frightened him. "No. You tell me, okay?"

She shook her head. "I'm not allowed."

It felt like someone was walking on his grave. "Why not?"

"You're not her family."

He shot off the chair, anger rising like flood waters against a levee. "I be all da damned family she got. What be going on?"

Tammy glanced at the hallway before facing him again. "No one can know I told you, or I'll lose my job." Her eyes filled. "They discontinued her treatments... and they placed her on a list for an organ transplant. If one doesn't become available very quickly, Molly might... Molly might not make it."

Mick's hand was shaking as he gently touched the girl's head. "Den we gotta go get one, right now."

"It's... it's not that simple."

He turned quickly to face her. "Den I'll make it happen. Jus' tell me how. If it be a money thing, I'll pay. Any price. Every penny I got to make it happen."

"I'm afraid you can't do anything for her because you're not family. And no, it's not about the money."

"An' if we were family, what could I do?"

Tammy swallowed hard before continuing. Mick listened carefully to what Tammy told him. After she left, he leaned down to kiss the baby's bald head. "Molly, I make you dis promise. You an' me, we'll find a way. Jus' hang in der'. Mick'll make it all right." He wiped moisture from her head, from the tears that fell from his cheeks.

***

Brenda's heart was full. Her baby was on the sofa, snuggled tightly against the man she loved. The movie, *A Christmas* Story, had just finished, again. Brenda glanced at her little girl. Didi was fast asleep. Luke wasn't far behind. *From the travel.* "Hey, you two. Maybe you better head to bed."

Didi stirred. "Yeah, guess I am a little tired. Getting up early every morning wears on me." Didi turned to Luke. "Why don't you head upstairs? I'll be along shortly and stop by to say goodnight. I promise."

The young man stood and stretched. "That's a good idea." He turned to face Brenda. "I really enjoyed watching the movie with you. Thanks for sharing your family traditions with me. 'Night, everyone." He headed up the stairs.

Warm arms wound around Brenda's waist. The fragrance of plumeria, Didi's perfume, filled her. Her daughter hugged her tightly and the whisper was soft, but loud enough for Brenda to hear. "What do you think of Luke?"

Brenda turned and smoothed an errant ripple in Didi's hair. "He's great. I like him. Dad does, too, despite teasing him a whole lot. The bigger question is, what do you think of this young man?"

Her daughter's eyes sparkled. "He's the one, Mom. Remember the stories you read to me when I was a little girl? How the prince would rescue the damsel in distress?" Her girl squeezed her hands. "The story came true, for me. He's my Prince Charming... my happily-ever-after."

Brenda touched her daughter's face, then turned to smile at Phil. "We know."

Didi brushed her mom's cheek before hugging and kissing her father. The pair watched their little girl head upstairs. Phil walked over and held his wife. "Isn't it great to have our family together?"

Brenda nodded. "Just like old times. Want some hot chocolate before we turn in?"

Phil winked. "Sure. You make it and I'll grab us some cookies."

After their snack, they snuggled, just watching the lights on the tree. Every ornament was something special. Most of them were handmade, by the three of them. Brenda's head was nodding when she heard footsteps on the stairs. She turned and watched as Luke walked until he stood before them.

"Sorry to bother you so late, but I wanted to make sure Didi was asleep before I came down. May I speak with you?"

Phil motioned to the stuffed chair. "Sure. What's on your mind? Need something to eat or drink?"

Luke squirmed. "No, sir, but thank you anyway." He swallowed hard before continuing. "First, I wanted to thank both of you for your hospitality."

Brenda smiled. "You're quite welcome."

Luke was silent as he took them in. "I'm, I'm in l-l-love w-w-with your daughter and, uh, I th-th-think she feels the same way."

Phil leaned forward. "Okay."

"I, uh, I hope this comes out right."

Brenda shared a concerned look with Phil. "Is something wrong?"

The young man shook his head. "No, no. Nothing like that. It's just we live so far away and we're only here for a short time. Uh... I need to ask you something." He stopped.

Oh my goodness! He's going to ask! "Go on, Luke."

"I love Didi."

Phil stifled a laugh while sporting his best poker face. "You're repeating yourself. What did you want to ask?"

Luke slicked his hair back and sat down. "I know you've only just met me, but I-I wanted to a-a-ask..." His hands were shaking.

Phil's voice was calm. "You're among friends, Luke. Ask away."

Luke balled his fists and closed his eyes momentarily. "I wanted to... to ask... ask if you'd mind... if it would be okay... if you wouldn't mind..." He sat tall in the seat. "I have a house I've renovated. It's just a house, except when D-D-Didi visits. When she's there, it, uh, becomes a home."

Brenda could sense the merriment in Phil's eyes. Her husband continued to tease the young man. "That's not a question. Do you have one?"

The young man took a deep breath and the words he spoke came out very fast. "Do I have permission to ask your daughter to marry me?"

Joy filled Brenda's heart. She glanced at her husband. His lips were clamped tightly together and his face held a stoic expression.

Phil cleared his throat. "And what can you offer her?"

Luke's eyes grew wide. "I, uh, have a house."

"She has a home, here, and an apartment in Pennsylvania. Anything else?"

The boy's chin was trembling. "I'll, uh, always keep her, um, well-fed and clothed and, she'll, like, never want for anything."

Phil shook his head. "Luke, anyone can give her 'things'. My little girl deserves better. Is this the best you can do?"

Brenda pinched her husband's leg and hissed. "Stop being mean!"

He shot her an angry look. "The woman he wants to marry is our daughter, our baby, our miracle. Do you remember?"

"Of course I do."

"Our girl deserves something special, and…"

Lucas stood and this time he didn't stutter. "Mr. Phillips, I love Didi. I promise to give her my undying love and devotion, and all my heart. I will always put her first. She's my world and I've got to tell you something. If you turn me down, I'll just keep asking. I need Didi like I need oxygen. Sir, I'll never give up. May I have your permission to propose to Deidre?"

Phil sat back and studied him. "Did she know you were going to ask?"

"No, sir."

"Hmm. And what will you do if I say no. Will you marry her anyway?"

Luke shook his head. "No, sir."

Phil's eyes opened wider. "No? Why?"

"Because I know how much Didi loves both of you. I'd never do anything to risk driving a wedge between you."

Her husband studied the young man. *I'm convinced.* "Phil?" The man she'd shared her entire life with turned to her. Their eyes met and she could see it. *We just gained a son.* Brenda nodded her head, ever so slightly.

Phil stood and turned to the boy. Luke remained tall and proud as he waited. Her husband extended his hand. "That's better. Welcome to the family, son."

Luke pulled Phil close and hugged him, then engulfed Brenda. "Thank you, both of you."

Phil cracked a smile and shook his head. "Might need to get your eyes checked, because, once again, I find you hugging my wife. We'll have to work on this."

A sleepy voice interrupted the party. "What's going on down here?"

They all turned to find Didi standing at the bottom of the stairs. She covered her mouth to hide her yawn.

Out of the corner of her eye, Brenda saw Luke's face. It was blood red. The boy's words were high-pitched. "H-how long were you standing there?"

Didi scratched her head. "I just came down to give you your phone. It's been beeping like crazy. I walked to your room to make sure everything was okay. When I saw you were gone, I decided to check down here." Didi stuck her arm straight out and offered him the phone. "Must be important."

Luke was reaching for the device when it rang. He answered, but didn't say another word. His eyes grew large. "Are you sure? Yes, sir. Day after tomorrow. I understand. I will be there."

Didi seemed fully awake now. She touched Luke's arm. "Everything okay?"

He grimaced. "No. We need to turn on the TV, now."

Chapter 18

E mma stepped out of the rental car. *This better be real important.* Since she had a key, she unlocked the door and entered Mick's house. Inside, it was a wreck. Dirty dishes filled every available space. She walked into the kitchen to find her brother slumped over, drinking coffee. "Well, ya texted, told me to come and said it was an emergency. What's so wrong?"

He turned and her heart went out to him. A bandage covered his forehead, but the most disconcerting thing was the look in his eyes. "Oh, Emma." He stood and quickly wrapped his arms around her. "My world's done gone to hell."

She had trouble breathing until he released her. "Mikey, what's wrong with you?"

His eyes were watery. "Everythin'."

"What happened to your head?"

"Got slashed wid a stick. But that don't matter."

Emma could feel the waves of despair rolling off of him. "Is something wrong between you and Riley?"

He rubbed his nose with the back of his hand. "We be through. She picked da job over me. In L.A."

Her eyes opened, wide. "What? When did that happen?"

"Christmas Eve."

Shock rippled through her body. "And you waited 'til yesterday to text me?" She sat on a bar stool, facing her big brother.

"Didn't want to ruin yer holidays." Mick sat and stared into his coffee cup. "I asked her ta be my wife, an'... an' she said yes."

Emma shook her head. "What? I thought you two broke up? Didn't you..." She halted, watching his lips quiver.

"She said yes, but den she tells me she be takin' a job in Los Angeles. And den she said she wanted time ta think 'bout where I be fittin' in. Here I thought she be in love wid me."

"So you're saying she broke up with you?" Emma touched the back of his hand. "I guess neither of us knew her. Riley seemed to be so in love with you. Thought she'd have second thoughts about Molly, but... she took a job on the other side of the country? And that's why she ended it with you?"

"No. I broke up wid her. Got mad when she handed me back dat ring. Threw the damned ting away. It be useless widout bein' on her finger, eh?"

Emma's mouth dropped open. "Are you a fool? You spent over fifteen thousand dollars on a ring and you just threw it away? Man, the great Mickey Campeau must be made of money."

"It's just a lump o' metal."

"Sure. A lump of metal with a diamond big enough to buy half of Canada. I'm concerned about your thinking. Chucking that ring like it was worthless, but more importantly, maybe you pressed her too hard." Emma rubbed his arm. "You need to be making it up to her. Both of us know how much you love Riley."

"Not no more. An' den der's this t'ing with Molly."

His eyes reddened. Creepy feelings worked up Emma's back. "What's wrong with Molly?"

"Dat damned cancer. Treatment's don't work. Dey stopped 'em." Mick swiped his nose on his arm. "Poor li'l Molly, she gonna die widout a liver transplant. Because she be an orphan, dey ain't gonna find one fer her. An' she ain't even got nobody der fer her." He stood, turned and then gripped Emma's arms tightly. "Dat's why I wanted you to be here." He grew silent as his eyes searched her face.

"Mikey, I live in Tennessee, not here. That's where my husband and my life are. If you're thinking that I'd move..."

Mick shook his head. "That's not why I asked ya to come. I need another favor." The big man's hands were shaking almost uncontrollably.

All her life, her brother had been the rock, so sure, so confident. Seeing him like this all but tore her heart out. "What can I do for ya, brother?"

"Come see da lawyer man wid me."

"A lawyer? Why?"

"I wanna adopt Molly, but the lawyer, he thinks I be crazy. Gotta convince him for me dat dis is what I really want."

"But why would you adopt a child if she's gonna die?"

The fire in Mick's eyes scared her. She hadn't seen his anger this strong since he'd walked in on the home invasion years ago.

"If I be her daddy, I can talk for her. Can make dem see how much she want ta live. We be gettin' her dat liver she gotta have. She needs me, Emma."

She held her brother again. *You were always there for me. I guess it's my turn now.* "I understand. Of course I'll come. I'll always be on your side."

"I need that li'l girl."

Emma patted his back. "I know. Let's come up with a game plan. Together, you and me, we can do anything, eh?"

***

Mick sat at the table in the judge's chamber, Emma to his right and the lawyer to his left. The judge was a tired looking lady with gray hair. She took off her glasses and looked directly in his eyes. "Explain to me again why you wish to adopt Molly."

Before he could respond, the lawyer answered, "My client is concerned about the welfare of this child. He's grown quite close to her over the last couple of months and wishes to make the little girl his daughter. And..."

The judge held her finger up to interrupt. "I read the application, but I didn't ask *you*. I asked Mr. Campeau." She now pointed her finger directly at Mick.

"Yer honor. Dat li'l girl, she ain't got no one. Nobody ta stand up fer her rights. Nobody to talk fer her."

The judge nodded. "Quite noble, but I don't think that's a solid enough reason. Adopting a child requires more than feeling sorry for her plight. I know her prognosis isn't exactly promising, but suppose she does pull through. Why should I consider your request?"

Judge don't believe me. If he was on the ice and she was a man, he'd pull her robe over her head and beat her senseless. *But we ain't on the ice and she be a lady.* Mick looked her in the eyes. "Ma'am, you can believe me or not, I don' care. I love that baby. Somethin' deep inside me tells me she needs me, an' know what? I need her, too. Life's been purty good to me. I got enough money to give her anythin' she ever be wantin'."

The judge looked away and shook her head. "Mr. Campeau..."

His anger was rising. *Already made up yer mind, eh?* "I can also give Molly somethin' else that she ain't got. I can give her love and a family."

"I don't doubt you feel that way, but look at this through the eyes of the court. You're a single man. And you're on the road quite often. Who will care for her when you're gone?"

Emma suddenly stood. "I will. My brother and I, we're a great team."

The judge pushed herself back from the table. "Mrs. Evans, I believe you live in Tennessee. How will you accomplish that? Are you willing to move here, with your brother so this child can have a stable life?"

Mick noted Emma's wince.

"Yes, if that's what's needed," she said.

Emma don't really want to do that, but because I'm her brother... It all became clear. *It's 'cause of me playin' hockey.* Mick patted his sister's hand.

"T'ank you, Emma, but that ain't gonna happen. You got a husband and a life down der. Sit down." He turned to the judge. "You don' think I be serious, eh?"

"Mr. Campeau, I don't think you've really thought this through. The welfare of this child is what's most important in the eyes of the court. Without a stable family unit, this situation is doomed for failure. Much of your life is spent on the road. What kind of an existence would that really be for Molly?"

The strong always protect the weak. His father's words. Mick's body relaxed, now that he'd accepted his fate. "Den I'll quit hockey. This baby, she be what's important ta me."

Emma gasped and then touched his arm. "But you love hockey. Always been your dream, eh?"

"Not no more. If bein' wid Molly be what's needed, I'll gladly do it. Like Daddy said, us strong ones gotta take care of da weak."

The judge slowly shook her head. "Are you listening to yourself, Mr. Campeau? You would give up your career for this child? Are you serious? Don't do something you'll regret to try and sway my opinion. Even if you do give up your career to be a stay-at-home father, I may still deny the request. Now, answer my question. Knowing the facts, would you still give up your profession?"

"Damn right. You be watchin' da news tomorrow. Soon as I leave here, I be quittin'. Molly needs me 'n I need her. Let my actions be showin' you." Mick stood and wagged a finger in the judge's face. "An' if'n you don't let me adopt her, I plan on bein' by dat li'l girl's side 'til da very end and you can't do nothin' to stop that. Good day, Judge." Mick turned and stormed off, Emma hot on his heels.

***

Hannah's head was spinning as she boxed up cookies for Saturday's farmer's market. *Didi Phillips-Zinn?* She couldn't believe her friend was now married. *Something's not right.* This morning was the first Didi had been on the news since before the holiday. And despite her smile before the camera, Hannah could feel her friend's despair. And then she signed off as *Didi Phillips-Zinn.*

Hannah glanced at the clock. She'd texted Didi to get the scoop, and Didi had replied she would tell her everything when she stopped by this afternoon.

The bell on the door sounded. Before Hannah could find her way to the counter, Didi came in through the swinging doors and wrapped her arms around Hannah. She was sobbing. "Missed you so much."

Hannah hugged her back. "Good afternoon, *Mrs. Zinn.* Are you really married?" Didi nodded and held out her hand. A modest engagement ring and a shiny wedding band were on her left ring finger. "This is so sudden. Where's your... husband?"

Didi wiped her eyes. "On his way to the Middle East."

Chills ran down Hannah's spine, as if someone had drenched her with a bucket of ice water. "Middle East? I don't understand."

Didi found a stool before palming her nose with the base of her hand. "Did you see what's happening over there, with the war breaking out?"

Oh no. "I did."

"Luke's unit deployed last night."

"Is that why you're suddenly married? I mean, Luke told us he was going to ask your parents' permission, but..."

Didi sniffled. "Yes."

"And he decided to marry you before he left? So suddenly?"

Her friend grasped her hands. "No. It was my idea."

"What?"

Didi fought off a sob. "I wanted to make sure he'll come back to me. If he knows he has a wife waiting for him, maybe he'll be more careful."

"Oh honey, I'm sure he'll be fine."

Didi shook her head. "Luke's dad always criticizes him for not being a real soldier, a hero. I'm scared he'll do something incredibly stupid, like trying to become a hero in his father's eyes."

Didi broke down and Hannah held her. She never would've predicted feeling so protective of someone she once viewed as competition, but now? "So, tell me about the ceremony."

"It wasn't much. He got the call to report to duty. We turned on the TV to watch the news. He told me that he'd asked my mom and dad's permission to propose. Something inside me told me we couldn't wait... so I proposed to him, and, and told him we needed to get married right away."

"What did your folks say?"

"Daddy wasn't happy, but Mom understood, after I explained it all to her. She supported me." Didi held out her hand. "This engagement ring belongs to her. She took it off her hand and gave it to Luke. Told him to put it on my finger, until we can get a real one, when he returns."

Hannah brushed her hair. "And he will."

Didi didn't seem to notice. "My parents gave us their room for our, our wed... our wedding night." Hannah rubbed her arm. Didi's cheeks were wet. "Luke and I decided we'll have a big ceremony when he gets home." Didi held Hannah's hands tightly. "Will you be my maid of honor? You're my best friend, after Luke."

Poor kid. "Of course, I'd be honored." *Need to do something to cheer her up.* "Hey, why don't you join us tonight, for dinner? Sam and our daughters are going to meet me at Shady Maple."

Didi wiped her cheeks. "You wouldn't mind?"

"Not at all."

"You're such a wonderful friend. Can I ask one favor, though?"

The look of hopefulness on the blonde's face was apparent. "Sure, anything."

"Can you and Sam help me move? I'm moving into Luke's, er, our house. I'm moving home. To Paradise." Didi dropped her gaze to the floor, then muttered, "By myself."

Chapter 19

R iley entered her new office and powered up the computer. She was in the process of logging on when her boss rushed in and parked his bottom on a chair. "Wow, do we have the story of the century. And guess who has the edge on everyone else? *Us.*"

Something about his expression sent a chill up her spine. The man's energy was almost rabid compared to how he'd been during the job interview. "What story?" she asked.

He winked. "You know..."

His look creeped her out. "Bill, I don't have a clue what you're referring to."

He nodded at her terminal. "Yes, you do. Open up the link I sent you, and start with the file from the other channel. I'll wait."

Her boss was staring at her intensely. She opened her account and selected the latest email. There were two videos attached. She opened the first one, from the competitor. When the clip started to play, Riley's mouth went dry. She watched the entire news conference before facing him. "I, uh, don't know what to say. Mickey Campeau just, he just quit hockey? Without an explanation?"

The man's smile unnerved her. "Oh, there's an explanation. And we have the exclusive. It's ours because I paid good money for it. Go ahead. Open the other attachment."

Her hands trembled as she directed the cursor over the second link and depressed the mouse button. Riley's mouth dropped open when she realized it was a phone video of *her* and Mick arguing. When he'd thrown her engagement ring into the night, Christmas Eve. Riley opened her mouth but nothing came out.

Bill's smile was ear to ear. "We are the only ones who know why hockey's greatest superstar quit the sport. Gave up his profession. And that's because you broke up with him. What better way to drive us to the top of the rankings than this great exclusive?"

Her hair was beginning to stand on end. "What?"

The manager laughed. "One of the reasons I hired you, Ms. Espenshade, was because you and Mr. Hockey were an item. He's nothing but a playboy. And I knew sooner or later, he'd dump you." The man was almost salivating. "Knew I'd get the exclusive. And think how lucky you are, Riley. You have the opportunity to drag him through the mud. I just never imagined it'd be so soon. Wow! What a way to make a name for our network."

The air in the room was suddenly hard to force into her chest. "You, you want me to... to make a fool of Mickey?"

Bill leaned back in the chair. "You got it, babe. Every wronged woman's dream. But you have the upper hand. You get to bury him on national television."

It was getting hard to see. *I wasn't hired for my talent, it was only because of my relationship.* "I... I can't do that."

The smile turned into a frown. "What do you mean, 'you can't do that'? Need I remind you, you signed a contract with us just last week to report the story? In this case, the story behind the story is yours to tell, in first person."

"Please, no. I'd never... I couldn't. I still love him."

"Yeah, right." Bill grew silent as he studied her reaction. "I'm beginning to wonder how much of a team player you are." He stood and looked down on her. "You need to think this through, Riley. Who will you be when you grow up? Want to be the top anchor on the hottest sports network or would you rather be some evening sportscaster back in Redneck, Pennsylvania?"

"Please don't make me do this. You can't run that video. I... it was a personal moment, just between the two of us, not something for the entire world to see."

Her boss slammed his hands on the desk. "It's drama and that's what makes headlines. You'll do this or I'll demote you to covering middle school dodgeball games. Think it through. You want a career as our anchor or not?" He left, slamming the door behind him.

Riley covered her mouth. "Oh God, what do I do?"

***

Mick sat holding Molly's hand. Emma was next to him, rubbing his back. The little girl's eyes seemed glued to him. It was easy to see the pain in her pale face. "It be okay, li'l one. I be here wid ya'."

"And your aunt Emma's here, too, baby girl."

Mick's voice was soft. "T'ank you fer bein' here, sis. Don't know if'n I could do this alone."

Emma's head was warm as she placed it on his shoulder. "Wish I could do more."

"Ahem." Brother and sister turned to see the man at the door. He slowly walked until he stood next to them, looking down on the girl. "How is she?"

"She be hurtin', lawyer man. Why you be here?"

He turned to face them with a sad smile. "Came to give you the good news. The judge approved the adoption. Congratulations. You're now a daddy."

Mick closed his eyes as he stood. *T'ank you, Big Man.* He leaned over and kissed Molly's head. "I be your daddy now, Miss Molly Campeau."

"There's paperwork to be signed before it's official. I made an appointment for tomorrow morning with the judge." He turned to Emma. "There is one condition. The judge wants you there, too. She'll allow this only if you will agree to be the maternal influence for the child. Are you willing to do that?"

Emma wiped her cheeks. "Damn right, I will."

After the lawyer departed, Mick lifted the girl from the bed, ever careful not to foul the IV lines. "I promise you, li'l one, I be doin' everythin' in my power to git you better."

Molly reached her hand up and rubbed it against his stubbles. A knock came at the door. A man in a white lab coat waited in the hall. *The doc. Good, need to talk to him. He be next on my list.* Mick pressed his lips to the girl's forehead before gently setting her down on the mattress.

Both Emma and Mick walked into the passageway to meet him. Mick got right to the point. "I be her daddy now... well, will be tomorrow. Time to get the ball rollin'. Molly needs ta get better, real soon, you gettin' me?"

The physician shook his head. "I understand that, Mr. Campeau. But the fact remains that Molly has a very rare type of cancer. Children normally don't get liver cancer, but she did. The child needs an organ transplant. Unfortunately, with her condition and prognosis, she's not high on the list."

Mick felt like punching him. "Den what we gotta do to git her to da top?" Unconsciously, Mick took a step toward the doctor.

The white-coated man moved away. "We, uh, might be able to get a living donor quicker."

Emma answered quickly. "What do you mean?"

"If we can find someone willing to donate part of their liver, and if they're a match, there's a chance it might work. Unfortunately, there's not a donor available right now."

Da strong always take care of da weak. Mick rubbed his chin. "I got a liver, right?"

The man eyed him curiously. "Of course you do. But..."

Hope was starting to build. "Den take part of mine."

"It's not that simple. First, we'd have to determine if your liver would be compatible with Molly's body, then..."

"How you figure dat out?"

"We'd start with a simple blood test."

Mick rolled up his sleeve. "Here ya go. Take my blood. Let's get crackin'." The doctor stared as if Mick had four heads. "Got somethin' in yer ears? I be talkin' to you, boy."

Pure fear covered the doctor's face. "Okay. I'll get someone from the lab up here right away, but don't get your hopes up. Your liver may not be compatible."

Emma stepped forward and exposed her arm. "In that case, you best be checking mine, too. That little girl isn't just Mikey's daughter, she's my niece, as well."

The doctor just stared at both of them, apparently at a loss for words.

Mick poked the man's chest with a forefinger. "Get movin', doc, or maybe ya want me to be lightin' a fire under you, eh?"

"O-okay." The man turned and headed to the nurse's station. "Don't go away."

"I be right here. Now git movin'."

***

Riley knocked on her boss's door. "Come in."

Opening the door seemed to take all her strength. "Bill, can we talk?"

"Depends. You ready to go public with this?"

No, there's no way. "Look, is there any way we can work this out so you *don't* run the clip from the party?"

His frown was menacing. "Tell me you're kidding. This is hot! Don't you realize we have the exclusive on him? And I paid a hundred grand for that video. This is something any scorned woman would absolutely love to do. You can get back at the man who dumped you."

Riley shook her head. "No, no. I can't do that to him. He's just mad right now, that's all. We're going to work it out. What would it take not to disgrace both of us?"

His face was red and he stood, looking down on her. "I am running with this story, either with Riley Espenshade taking the lead or with her benched." He clenched his fists in apparent frustration. He stepped menacingly toward Riley. "Know what? Just go home. And I want you to spend tonight thinking about what you want to do with your career. Either you lead with this story tomorrow or your days as an anchor here—or anywhere else, for that matter—are over."

It was a struggle just to get back to her office. Riley was shaking all over as she collected her purse. *I need to warn Mick.* Before she even got to the car, she dialed his number. But just like every time she'd called since Christmas Eve, it went straight to voicemail. "Mickey, it's Riley. Please call me. This is urgent. I need to warn you about something. Please, please call me back. If not for me, for your sake."

Sitting behind the wheel, she wracked her mind to find a way to get hold of him. *Emma!* If he

159

wouldn't listen to Riley, he might listen to his sister. Riley quickly pulled up Emma's number, but it also went straight to her mailbox.

"God, please help me. I need a miracle."

Chapter 20

"Okay, I'll be there at midnight. You sure we can get across the border without being caught? Great. I'll have the money, don't you worry." Kyle could barely contain his smile. Months of planning were about to pay off. *See what them Campbells and that Hannah think after this. Payback's here.*

It was time to get in position. Luckily Edmund's nightly round would be after dark, so Kyle could arrive at his ambush location without detection. He'd buried the sled to move Edmund's body under dead pine boughs months ago.

Forty minutes later, Kyle was hunkered down, the scent of pine bolstering his courage. Every cell in his body was on alert. There was no wind, just a cold, dark night with a heavy, overcast sky. Kyle checked the device, making sure it was ready for action.

The strain of someone whistling a tune he didn't recognize caught his attention. Kyle peeked through the branches. *Right on schedule.* Edmund Campbell approached, wearing only a light jacket. It wasn't zippered. *Perfect.* His victim walked past the copse of trees so he could inspect the entire length of the hot house. Kyle stepped out, completely prepared as he pulled his hood close to cover his features. With a cane in his left hand, Kyle was hunched over like an old man.

He imitated an elderly voice as he called out to the young Scotsman, "Sonny, can you help me? I'm lost."

Edmund quickly turned. Twenty feet separated them as Edmund stepped closer. "What in blazes are you doing—"

Kyle made his move, throwing away the cane and pointing the weapon with his right hand. Even in the gloom, Kyle could see the color drain out of his victim's face. *He recognized me, but it's too late. Gotcha.* Kyle squeezed the trigger and laughed as Edmund's body fell to the ground.

***

Hannah hugged Didi and watched her drive off into the night while her family was inside, throwing their coats into a pile. Hannah closed the door to find Missi rubbing her eyes and Beth yawning. "Time for bed, you two."

Sam swept his youngest in his arms. "Come on, Moana. Let's brush your teeth while Mommy picks out a book."

Hannah turned to Beth. "You want to join us?"

Beth shook her head. "I think I'll call it a night. Five o'clock was awfully early."

Hannah touched her cheek. "This was nice of you to go along with Sam today. Tomorrow, the three of us will go to the tea room while Sam tends the stand at Bird-in-Hand, okay?" Beth nodded. "I love you, sweetheart."

Beth hugged her mother. "Love you, too, Mom. Give Sam a kiss for me." The teenager headed up the stairs.

Hannah was waiting when Sam carried Missi to bed. The three of them snuggled as Sam read Dr. Seuss's *Oh, the Places You'll Go*. Missi was asleep before page five.

Sam closed the book and kissed his daughter's forehead. Hannah followed suit and pulled the door softly behind her. At the bottom of the stairs, her husband waited, lifting her in the air as he twirled her around, his lips on hers.

He pulled away. "You're so beautiful, Hannah."

She shook her head and giggled. "Not yet. We still have to load the truck before we head to bed."

Sam winked at her. "Darn. Let's hurry."

He backed the truck up to the rear of the shop next door. Hannah pulled the dolly out and the pair worked as a team, loading the crates of cookies, cakes and pies into the box truck. They were almost done when a blood-curdling scream rent the night. "Help! Mom, Sam! The house is on fire!"

Hannah and Sam ran toward the house. As they rounded the corner, Hannah's heart almost stopped beating. Flames filled every window of the first floor, as well as several on the second floor. When she caught sight of Beth's image backlit by flames, Hannah screamed.

***

Sam grabbed Hannah's arms. "Call 911! I'll go get our girls." Despite his crooked leg, Sam ran faster than ever before. He grabbed the knob on the screen door, but immediately yanked away. The fire had heated the metal handle, and now his right palm was missing skin.

He stepped back and grasped his cane like a baseball bat. A quick swing shattered the pane of glass. Using the crook of his instrument, he ripped the door from its frame. A glance through the window revealed a fiery hell awaiting. *My girls need me. God, I need help.* Sam didn't hesitate. He slammed his shoulder against the oak portal. It didn't budge, but finally gave way on attempt number six.

Sam wasn't prepared for the quick release, and his momentum carried him over the threshold. He landed on the flaming lump of combustibles that used to be his easy chair. The intensity of the heat was overwhelming. Forcing himself to his feet, Sam realized his shirt was on fire.

A dark figure contrasted against the wall of flame. Sam's lip quivered when he recognized the face. A screaming voice filled his ears. *"You're on fire, Scooter! Drop and roll."* Without question, Sam followed Jenna's directions. Within seconds, the flames were extinguished. Jenna's hands were on his shoulders. *"Get Missi to the roof and hand her down to Hannah. Follow me!"*

This can't be happening. Did I die? He followed his sister, running the gauntlet of fire. Jenna seemed to know the way to Missi's room. She turned at the top of the stairs and disappeared through the door into the young girl's room. Sam followed, but had to kick the door in.

Missi was standing on top of her mattress, hands over her ears as she screamed. Jenna stood next to the little girl, staring at her. Missi opened her arms and reached for Sam. "Daddy, I'm scared!"

He took his baby in his arms and held her tight. "It's okay, Missi, I gotcha." He turned to the door. Flames were storming behind him, charring the carpet.

"Scooter! Get Missi to the roof and hand her down to Hannah."

Sam pulled Missi tightly to his chest and took off for the window. Just before slamming into the glass, he turned his face away. His shoulder destroyed the pane and he was suddenly laying in the snow on the roof. The freezing cold night air was soothing.

Jenna stood beside him, hands on her hips. *"Get moving! You still have to rescue Beth."*

Sam forced himself to his feet. "Hannah! Where are you?"

"Here! Here! Do you have Missi?"

"Yes. I'll hand her down." Missi was shaking uncontrollably in his arms. He kissed her head. "It'll be fine, baby. You go to Mommy now." He held her hands and lifted her out over the rain gutter.

Hannah stood below, arms raised above her head. "I've got you, sweetheart."

The height of the roof was too great. He would have to drop Missi. "Wait, Hannah. Let me get her closer." He wriggled closer to the periphery, trying to lower the screaming child to his wife. *A little more...* His hips were at the edge. Then he felt it. He started to slide over the edge when his belt suddenly tightened, as if someone was gripping it.

"I've got her," Hannah called. "Let go, Sam." Sam released his hold, watching Hannah stumble backwards, before dropping to the ground while holding the little girl. She rapidly nodded her head. "She's safe!"

Some force pulled at his hips and Sam found himself standing on the roof. He pointed to the side of the house and yelled to Hannah, "Meet me over by Beth's room." Hannah nodded. In the distance, his vision captured the flashing red lights as help approached. But when he turned to the window he'd shattered, he hesitated. Flames were shooting out.

Another force yanked at his arm. He turned to see Jenna's face right next to him. *"Come on, let's go!"* His feet were frozen to the snow. But Jenna shoved him, then pointed inside. *"If you don't go right now, your other daughter will die. The brother I loved wouldn't hesitate even one second. Get moving. I'll be right next to you."*

Sam leapt through the window, ignoring the conflagration around him. Turning left in the hallway, he charged right through Beth's door. His eldest was curled in a fetal position near the window. The cuff of her pajamas was burning.

Sam hit his knees and smothered the flames with his bare hands. Beth's eyes were open wide, but she didn't move. He grabbed her vanity chair and destroyed the window, using the legs to clear the remaining fragments. "Beth, help me. I'll hold your hands and lower you to Mom."

The girl's eyes were vacant and she didn't move, even when he shook her. He scooped her in his arms and leaned out the window where Hannah was waiting below.

His wife stretched her arms toward her daughter. "Drop her, I'll catch her."

Jenna's voice whispered in his ear. *"It's too far. You'll hurt her, or Hannah, if you let go now."*

"Sam, drop her!"

Jenna was right. *I can't risk it.* "I saw the fire truck approaching. Have them help you."

Hannah turned and ran to the screaming siren of the big fire truck. He remained leaning out of the window, where he could breathe in the cold winter air. The heat bearing down on him was almost unbearable, except for a sudden cool touch on his back.

"Hang in for just a couple more seconds, bro. I'm here with you, Scooter."

The pain was intense, but the horrible odor of burning meat was even worse. Sam knew the source was his own singed skin.

A voice seemed to come from far away. "Hey you, in the window. Let her go. We'll catch her."

Sam's eyes focused on the men below, the ones holding a tarp. He glanced at his daughter's face. Her eyes were fixated over his shoulder, to the source of the voice that whispered in his ear. *"You did it, Scooter. She's safe now. Let Beth go."*

Sam released his grip. As soon as he did, Beth grasped for him, but missed. He watched her body bounce twice before the firefighters helped her to Hannah's arms.

Everything was growing dim. Sam's legs seemed paralyzed. The men standing on the ground were screaming at him, but it was unintelligible. His eyes drifted to his wife. Her eyes locked on his. *Loved you the first moment I saw you.* Her lips were moving, but the noise of the fire was too loud. *Goodbye, Hannah.* Everything went dim.

***

Henry Campbell shivered in the cold night air. He was searching for his brother. Edmund's wife Tara had called earlier and said he hadn't arrived home for dinner. So being the eldest, Henry began the search. Within minutes, he discovered Edmund's truck parked in front of the office, but his brother was nowhere to be found. Henry immediately expected the worst. *I'll find you, Edmund. I promise you this, on my life.*

When he reached the copse of trees, Henry was puzzled. In the soft ground of the field, two parallel lines headed off into the distance. Someone had dragged something away. A quick search of the area revealed two other interesting items—a discarded cane and Edmund's phone. Henry ripped his own cell phone from his pocket, quickly dialing his other brother, Harry.

His brother answered with a laugh. "Henry."

"Listen. I need you to do this immediately. Get everyone into my house, pronto, then lock the doors. Tell Ellie I said to fully alarm the house, she'll know what to do. If anyone besides me tries to enter, you repel them, using whatever force necessary. Let Ellie know I said *you* are the man of the house until I return."

Harry was no longer laughing. "What happened?"

"Edmund disappeared. I'd bet my future that it involves Kyle Parker. I'm going to find him."

"What are you going to do?"

"Kyle and I are going to have a long heart to heart. Then, I'll do what I do best. I'm going to save the day." A whirring noise filled the air above him.

"I'll come with you."

"No. We don't know Parker's next move. He might strike at someone else in the family. I need you there, to protect everyone. You're the only one I trust."

The phone was momentarily silent. "Anyone who gets in will have to step over my dead body."

"I know. Go make me proud."

The noise came closer. Though Henry couldn't see it against the cloud covering, he knew it was a drone. The ringing of a mobile interrupted the silence of the night. Edmund's. The phone screen flashed 'Unknown Number'. But Henry knew exactly who it was. "Hello, Kyle, you scumbag."

A sinister laugh followed. "Henry Campbell. Guess who's here with me."

"I know you have my brother. What do you want?"

"First, beg for me to tell you."

Henry's vision was tinged with red. "I'm begging."

"No, you're not. I can see you. Get down on your knees."

Wait until I get my hands on you. Henry dropped to the ground. "Okay, I'm begging with bended knee. What do you want?"

"Money."

"Money? How much?"

"Every penny you have. You got one hour to meet me at my place. I've got surveillance cameras surrounding me. If I see one cop car, or if you bring anyone but yourself, your brother's done. You understand?"

"How in the world can I get together any amount of money tonight? I need more time."

"Bring your bank account numbers. That's all you need. I'll handle it from there."

"Fine. I'll be there in one hour."

"And one more thing. My drone's above you. Throw both those phones away, yours and Edmund's. If you stop anywhere but here, you'll never see your brother again... alive, that is. Got it?"

"Yeah."

"Yeah what?"

Henry trembled all over. *You just signed your death warrant, scum.* "Yes... *sir.*"

"That's better. Now, get moving."

Henry dropped both devices to the ground and headed for his truck. "You filthy bugger. You made a capital mistake, boy. You'll rue the day you messed with *my* family."

Chapter 21

H enry Campbell zipped his jacket before stepping out of the truck. A quick check of his surroundings revealed nothing out of sorts. He glanced at the roof and saw them. As Kyle had indicated, there were multiple cameras hung from the soffit. *My presence will keep the idiot occupied.* He walked to the door and knocked. The door slowly swung open from the pressure of his fist. Gagged and tied to a wooden chair was his brother, Edmund. Behind him stood Kyle, a long knife resting on Henry's brother's left shoulder.

Kyle grinned. "Lock the door and lose your coat." Henry did as told, throwing his jacket at Edmund's feet. "Empty your pockets and turn around so I can see you ain't got no weapons."

Henry did as instructed. "Okay. The door's locked and Edmund is tied to a chair in front of you. I did what you wanted. Now let my brother go. This is between you and me, and doesn't involve him."

Kyle laughed. "You think I'm stupid, don't ya?"

Yes, but that's beside the point. Henry stepped closer. Kyle lifted the sharp edge of the knife to Edmund's neck. "One step closer and I'll use this, understand?"

Need to draw him away from my brother. Henry took one step back. "Okay, Kyle. You're in charge. You've got a knife against my brother's neck. Now what?" Edmund's eyes questioned why he was stating the obvious. *You'll understand, very shortly.*

"Where's the bank account information?"

"It's in my head."

Kyle threw a pad and pencil at Henry. "Then write it down."

Henry noted the bag at Kyle's right side and how the man reached into it. Kyle's hand wrapped around something.

Got yourself a weapon, don't you? Henry picked up the pad and pencil, then hesitated. He glanced at his brother. Edmund's eyes motioned his intentions to Henry. *Perfect.*

"Did you hear what I said?"

"I did. I'll write it down as soon as you let Edmund go."

"Do it now, or else!" Kyle again lifted the knife.

Henry scribbled an obscenity on the pad. "Okay, I wrote it down. Let him go."

"Throw it here."

Henry looked at Edmund and nodded, ever so slightly. "Okay, Kyle, here you go. Throwing it to you now." Henry arced the tablet high in the air to the left of Kyle, and yelled, "Long live the Queen." Kyle instinctively dropped the knife to try and catch the tablet. At the same time, Edmund pushed off with his left foot, forcing the chair sideways onto the floor. Henry shot forward like a rocket.

Kyle reacted by reaching into the bag to grasp his weapon from it. He pointed the device at Henry and squeezed the trigger. Twin probes shot forward, but Henry was prepared. He turned sideways to limit his profile while windmilling his right arm. Henry caught the wires from the Tazer in his hand and yanked. Both probes pulled out of the device.

"Damn you," screamed Kyle as he dropped the weapon and reached for the knife. Kyle was still trying to get it in front when Henry ripped the blade from his hand and roughly shoved him to the floor. Then Henry threw the knife behind them.

He yelled, "Situation's under control. Edmund's safe. Parker's down."

Kyle looked confused. "Who are you talking to?"

The front door suddenly splintered and men in tactical gear rushed in, weapons pointed at Kyle. "Get your hands up and on your knees, now."

Kyle's eyes engaged Henry's. "Bastard! You double-crossed me!"

Henry laughed. "No, I did exactly as you requested. I threw away those two phones, but you forgot about my personal mobile. The one I keep in the truck for emergencies, like this one. I had it in my coat pocket, on speaker the whole time, so the police could listen in."

Edmund was struggling violently against his restraints. Henry retrieved Kyle's knife and severed the rope. As soon as Edmund's hands were free, he yanked the cloth from his mouth. "We need to get help. He set fire to Sam and Hannah's house!"

Henry whipped around to face his nemesis. Kyle just smiled. "Payback's a bitch, ain't it, Henry?"

***

Didi's hands were sweaty as she rushed into the hospital. The call from Riley had astonished her. *Poor Hannah.* Didi couldn't believe her friend's house had burned down. She'd almost fainted when Riley told her Hannah's entire family had been taken to the hospital. Riley begged Didi to go see them so Didi stopped at the information desk and asked where to find the Espenshades. The receptionist gave her a card with a room number.

One of the people in the elevator was hacking up a lung and Didi was grateful she only had to ride up one floor. She rushed down the hall, then stopped and said a brief, but intense prayer before pushing the door open.

Hannah's head turned and she stood when she saw who was there. Didi grabbed her friend in a tight hug. "What happened? Is everyone okay?"

Hannah looked shell-shocked. She swallowed hard and shook her head. "S-Sam, he's got he's got third-degree burns on his back and legs."

Didi glanced at the person in the bed, covered in sheets. "Is that him?"

Hannah wiped her arm across her cheek and looked at her husband. "Yeah."

Seeing her friend like this made Didi's eyes blurry. "Are Beth and Missi all right?"

Hannah slowly turned. "They're both in shock. Missi wasn't hurt, but Beth..." Hannah fought back a sob. "Beth has a nasty burn on her leg. If Sam... if he hadn't rushed into the flames and rescued them when he did, I might, I might..." Hannah was too emotional to continue for a while. Didi simply held her friend, waiting for her to continue. "I almost lost my entire family."

"How did the fire start?"

Hannah's face turned red. "The police came by earlier and told me it was arson. They said Kyle Parker set our house on fire."

Didi shuddered. "Kyle Parker? Isn't he the man who broke Sam's leg?"

"Yes. He bragged to the police it was payback, for me and Henry Campbell."

"Henry Campbell? What's Kyle have against him?"

Hannah wiped her hair away from her eyes. "Henry fired Kyle when he attacked me and broke Sam's leg."

Didi was confused. "How would setting your house on fire get back at Henry?"

"The police also said Kyle kidnapped Edmund. Henry and the cops freed him."

"What? Edmund is Tara's husband, right?"

Hannah nodded. "And Henry Campbell's brother." Hannah's eyes were intense as she gripped Didi's arms. "I know you won't believe me, but something really, really strange happened tonight. Beth told me she saw a woman in the house with Sam."

"A woman?"

Hannah nodded her head. "Beth said she recognized her from a picture hanging in Sam's parents' house."

"Who was it? Did she get out of the fire alive?"

Hannah was shaking all over. "Beth said it was *Jenna.*"

The sensation of spiders crawled up Didi's spine. "Jenna? Isn't that Sam's sister who died in the car crash? Riley told me about her."

Hannah brushed the hair from her eyes. "Sam once told me that Jenna's last words were that she would always be with him. B-Beth said she was there tonight, with S-Sam, in the house."

Hannah's losing it. "Are you sure?"

"You weren't there. After Sam dropped Beth to the firemen, he seemed to collapse against the window frame." Hannah wiped her cheeks. "I thought he was... that he'd died. Then, it looked like someone threw him out the window. I believe, I really believe..."

"Hannah?" The weak voice came from the man in the bed.

Hannah dropped to her knees and held his hand. "Sam. Sam, it's me. I'm right here."

"Hannah? Did, did they... are our daughters okay?"

Tears were dripping from Hannah's cheeks. "Yes, thanks to you. You saved them. Oh, Sam. I was so worried about you. You were so brave."

"Wasn't just me. *She* helped."

Hannah stood and glanced briefly at Didi. "Who helped you?"

He extended his arm and pointed to the empty space next to Hannah's side. "Her."

"I'm not sure who you mean."

His arm was shaking. "My sis, Jenna. Can't you see her? She's standing there, right next to you."

Didi glanced, but the room was empty apart from the three of them. The two women exchanged a confused look. "Nobody's there, Sam. You must be dreaming."

His arm fell to the bed. "She's here. Told me I couldn't go with her. Said you needed me too much."

Hannah knelt and kissed his hand. "Jenna's right. I need you desperately. I love you, Sam."

Didi could see his smile.

"Love you, too, Hannah." He raised his hand slightly. "Bye, Jenna." Sam drifted back to sleep.

***

Didi dialed Riley's cell. The tone of her friend's voice concerned her. It sounded like Riley had been crying. "Didi, Mom gave me an update, but I'm scared she's sugarcoating things. Give me the truth, how's my brother?"

"He'll be fine, in time."

"What do you mean in time?"

This is so hard. "Riley, Sam has third-degree burns over forty percent of his body."

Riley cried out. "Oh my God. Is he in much pain?"

"He's pretty sedated, but was kind of spaced out. It was really weird."

Riley was sniffling. "What was weird?"

"Sam, and the things he said. He told Hannah that Jenna helped him. And Beth told Hannah that Jenna had been there, in the burning room. Said your sister was standing beside Sam. Don't you find that odd?"

Riley hesitated. "No. Didi, there was a special bond between Sam and Jenna. Sam told me that after she died, Jenna talked to him. Told him she'd always be with him. If Sam said Jenna was there, I believe him."

What? "I g-guess, if you say so."

"Can we change the subject?"

Why? "Sure."

Riley sniffled. "Didi, I screwed up, *royally*. I need help."

The way her friend said the words sent a shiver across Didi's shoulders. "What happened?"

"I never should have taken this job in California. Biggest mistake I ever made. I should be there, in Lancaster, not in L.A."

Oh, that explains it. "It's okay, Riley. We've got it all under control. Your mom's watching the girls and I'll be there for Hannah."

"Thanks, but that's not what I'm talking about. There's more."

"Like what?"

Riley was crying. Didi waited. "If you need to talk, I'm here. What's going on?"

"They're, they're... trying to force me to smear Mick's name."

She shivered. Didi turned on the ignition in the car, trying to get some heat. "I don't understand."

"Did you see the press conference? Mickey quit the NHL."

"He what? I thought you said he loved hockey. Why would he leave the game?"

Riley sobbed hard. "Because of me."

"Riley, this isn't making sense."

Her friend didn't appear to hear her. "And, and the worst thing is... someone took a video of us arguing in the parking lot. My manager bought the clip and... and wants me to go public. Told me I need to make a fool out of Mick."

Didi was shaking. *From the cold or what Riley was telling her?* The temperature gauge was moving from blue toward the center of the dial. Didi turned on the heater. "Of course you're not going to do it, are you?"

"I tried to get a hold of Mickey to warn him, but he's got his damned phone turned off." Riley sobbed again. "This isn't worth it. I don't know what to do or where to go."

Her heart went out to her friend. "You can always move in with me."

"You'd take me in, back at the apartment?"

I have so much to tell you. "I, uh, cancelled the lease on the apartment."

"What? Why?"

"Because I'm moving into Luke's house, er, I mean, *our* house."

"Your house? Are you moving in together?"

"Kind of. But Luke isn't there."

"Where is he?"

Didi thought of Luke and wiped her eyes. "He's somewhere in the Middle East. His unit was deployed because of the war. I was so scared. Before he left, Luke and I got married."

Silence, dead silence followed. "Married? I'm sorry, Didi."

Sorry I married Luke? "Why would you be sorry about that? I proposed to him."

Riley's voice was shaky. "Not for that. I'm sorry for... well, for not being the friend to you I should have been. My life stinks. I can't do anything right. I lost Mickey, I lost my job, I wasn't there when my family needed me and I wasn't there for you. Screwed everything up. I'm, I'm... nothing."

Didi's voice was soft. "You're so wrong, Riley. You're my friend and that's something."

"Right. Some friend, huh?"

Didi sighed. "Do you remember last year, at Christmas? I was so messed up, being away from my family. But know what got me through? You did. I survived because of your friendship. Look, if you want to come back to Lancaster, plan on staying with me, okay? It'll be just like old times, and know this, my friend. I'll always be there for you."

Riley was sobbing. "After everything, are you sure you want me?"

Of course. "Absolutely. We're like sisters and I'm always here for you. Text me your flight information and I'll be waiting."

Riley drew a deep breath. "You're so kind. I'm gonna see how soon I can make it there. Thanks, Didi. I know we haven't been close lately, but..."

"Stop it. This is what friends do."

"All right. See you soon."

After Riley disconnected, Didi sat there, enjoying the heat in the car's cabin. Luke's face drifted before her eyes. *I wish it was you, coming home.*

Chapter 22

"Don't see how ya wear dis stuff all da time." Mick hopped up on the stretcher. "Kinda drafty down there, eh? An' dis thing be cold."

Emma messed up his hair. "Don't make fun of women's clothes." She stopped, looking into her brother's eyes. *He's scared, a little.* "It's gonna be fine."

Mick inhaled sharply. "'Course it'll be. An' me, I be real good. Jus' a walk in da woods. Now make sure dey let us see Molly 'fore the docs get to cuttin'."

She held his hand. "Sure ya wanna do this?" Mick nodded. "Even after the doctor said you should wait and get rid of the infection first?"

By the look in his eyes, she knew his resolve had hardened. Especially after the new sports channel ran a cell phone video of Mick and Riley's break-up from Christmas Eve. Emma knew he loved Molly... now, even more. Still, a twinge of fear worked itself up inside her. "You're a great man, Mikey Campeau. And I'm proud to call myself your sister, but putting this off a couple of days won't hurt."

Her brother's lips formed a fine white line across his face.

"And there's still the other option. Let them take part of my liver instead. I'm healthy as a moose."

"Now, we talked about dis before, eh? I'm Molly's daddy, and it be my responsibility to..."

"Save your breath. The doctor said there are big risks or else he wouldn't have made you sign the 'against medical advice' papers." Her eyes were suddenly blurry. Her next words were whisper quiet. "What am I gonna do if something happens to my big brother?"

Mick touched her cheek. "I be tougher den nails. Ain't nothin' bad gonna happen, wait an' see, eh?" He took her hand and kissed it. "But if it do go bad, ya gotta promise me you'll take gud care o' Molly. She needs us. Dat's why we can't wait."

Emma paused until she calmed down. "But you're sick, Mikey. Let them take mine in your place."

"No."

"I haven't ever asked for much, eh? But I'm asking now."

He shook his head. "Den don't ask, 'cause the answer be 'no'. The strong gotta..."

Emma's emotions caught up in her throat. "Quit saying that." She had to turn away briefly before continuing. "You always looked out for me. Please, let me look out for you, just this once, okay?"

"Absolutely no."

"Knock, knock." The head of one of the nurses popped in through the drawn curtain. "Are you ready, Mr. Campeau?"

"As ready as I'll ever be, eh?"

"Fine. Let me confirm your identity. Tell me your name and date of birth."

Emma forced herself to be tough, for her brother, not for her. She stayed by his side as they hooked up the IV. Two different doctors came to talk with him before the transport team arrived.

From deep within her heart, bad feelings began to surface. *God, please watch over him. I need my brother.*

One of the nurses turned to her. "I'm afraid you'll have to stay here."

Before she could answer, Mick spoke up. "I be wantin' Emma to come wid me, least as far as she can. An' I want her to talk wid Molly, to calm da girl down."

The nurse smiled, then nodded. Emma walked beside him, holding his hand. At the entrance to the operating room, they stopped. She kissed her brother's cheek. "You're the bravest man I've ever known. Love you. See ya in recovery."

He squeezed Emma's hand. "An' I be da luckiest man alive, ta have you be my sis. Love you, too. See ya on the other side, okay?"

Emma couldn't speak, but nodded. The operating room doors had no sooner closed when another stretcher appeared behind her. The pale little girl looked up at Emma and smiled. *So brave. Just like your daddy.* Emma kissed the girl's bald head and whispered, "Everything will be just fine, little girl. When you wake up, Aunt Emma's gonna be there."

Molly wrapped her hand around Emma's finger. Emma kissed her niece's head before removing her finger from the girl's grip.

She watched as the door swung shut again. Emma pawed at her eyes. The quick beat of footsteps running in the hallway behind her interrupted her thought.

A woman's voice called out. "Am I too late?" Emma turned and looked at the woman's face. Riley Espenshade stood before her.

"What the hell are *you* doing here?"

***

Didi was dead tired, but she continued to pour filling into the pie tins. *Hannah's my best girlfriend. I made a commitment.* Beth would arrive at the shop as soon as her choir practice was finished. Maybe the teenager would lend a hand.

The bell on the door tinkled. Didi used a cloth to wipe perspiration from her face as she prepared to greet the customer. But before she could move, the kitchen door swung open. *Hannah?* "Hi, what are you doing here?"

The older woman also looked worn out. "Hey, Didi. This is nice, you helping out, but I can't let you be stuck doing everything. After all, it is my business and I should be here."

Didi hugged her. "No. You should be with your husband. How was Sam's surgery?"

"It was okay. He's such a trooper." Hannah stopped to blow her nose. "They don't know yet how many more skin grafts he'll have to go through."

"I'm so sorry. You should be at the hospital, with your husband." *Wish I could be with mine.*

"His mom took over and I asked his dad to watch Missi. What has to be done yet?"

"This is the last batch of pies. The cookies and whoopee pies are all made and are ready to be packaged." Hannah stumbled when she moved to the sink to wash her hands. "You're running yourself ragged, lady." Didi grabbed a stool and pulled it to the big table. "Why don't you sit for a while?"

"Thanks, but only for a second. It's been a long day." Hannah's hands were trembling.

Her blood sugar's low. "When's the last time you ate?"

Hannah shrugged. "This morning, I guess."

"Then I'll get you something. I have half a sub left over from lunch. Would you like it?"

Hannah nodded. *Poor woman.* "That's so gracious. I'm afraid this is just too much, right now, with everything going on. Maybe I should shut the business down for a while."

"What? Nonsense. I'm here and I don't mind helping." Didi closed the refrigerator door and placed the sandwich and a bottle of soda in front of Hannah.

"You're a great friend, but I can't expect you to do this every day. You've got a real job, and it's demanding. I know you're tired. What time do you get up?"

"Two, but I really don't mind. With Luke being gone, I've got nothing better to do." She bit her lip to keep the sadness at bay. Having something to do passed the lonely hours.

Hannah took a bite of the food and watched as Didi ladled apple filling into the pies. "You're really good at that."

Didi smiled. "Learned from the best."

Hannah retrieved a paper towel to wipe her mouth. "Even so, without Sam, there's no way I can tend stand, bake goods and run the household. I've got to close for a while."

The bell again jingled. "No. Together, we can do anything," Didi said. "Hold that thought and we'll figure out a plan."

In walked Riley through the kitchen door. She looked terrible. "Hey. You okay?"

Sam's sister shook her head. "Not so much."

Hannah patted Riley's back. "When did you get back in town? What's wrong?"

"Ashley Campbell called me. She and her husband were in the children's cancer ward when they ran into Emma. Ash told me Mick was going into surgery today."

Didi and Hannah shared a concerned look. Simultaneously, they queried, "Surgery?"

Riley nodded. "Yep. Molly needs a liver transplant and he... he volunteered to be a living donor."

Didi handed her a bottle of chilled water. "Was the operation today?" Riley nodded. "Then why are you here? Shouldn't you be with him at the hospital?"

Hannah's face whitened. "Oh no. Did something happen? He is all right, isn't he?"

"I wouldn't know." Riley took a deep breath. "I was told to leave."

Hannah and Didi again exchanged a puzzled look. "Who told you that?" Hannah asked. "Mickey?"

Riley winced, hard. "Nope. His sister told me to get out of the hospital and stay away from her brother. Forever."

"Why would she do that?"

Riley sighed. "I take it you haven't seen the news."

Hannah shook her head, but Didi grimaced.

"Someone took a phone video, on Christmas Eve... when Mickey and I broke up. The media is having a field day with this. And Emma... Emma thinks I'm behind it. That I did it just to make a scene so I'd be famous. Emma told me I was nothing but a low-life, greedy gold-digging witch and to stay away from her brother."

Both women embraced Riley in a hug.

"But that's not true," Didi comforted. "You quit your job because of the story. You didn't sell him out."

"Emma thinks I did."

"Then we'll have to convince her otherwise. Maybe I should..."

"No, Didi. The timing wasn't right. Emma was so mad, I thought she was going to slug me. Said next time she saw me, she'd kick my butt."

"Oh, Riley. What can we do for you?"

Riley palmed her eyes. "Just being here, being a great friend... it means more than you'll ever know."

Hannah's eyes were wide. "I didn't know you quit your job. You just started."

"I had to. The new station wanted me to report on the break-up and make a master fool of Mickey. The producer said Mick was a playboy and needed to be put in his place. Told me if I wouldn't smear him, I couldn't be an anchor. So I did the only honorable thing. I quit."

Hannah pushed the hair back from Riley's eyes. "Tell me how I can help. I'd offer to let you move in with us, but... our home is gone. We're living with the Campbells right now."

Riley nodded. "I know. I'm moving back in with Didi. Mom told me about Kyle and the fire and... and how Sam almost died saving the girls." Riley's face was wet. "I'm so sorry I wasn't there for you. Taking that stupid job and leaving everything that was important... biggest mistake I ever made. I lost my job, the love of my life, everything. I wasn't there when you and Sam needed me. I'm the world's biggest failure."

Hannah held her hand. "Stop it. You're here now. What are you going to do? Maybe you can get your old job back."

"My pride won't let me." Riley pouted. "I quit with no notice. I let them down."

A light turned on in her mind. *I know!* Didi spoke. "There is something you can do, until you get everything figured out."

Riley sniffed. "What's that?"

Didi touched her shoulder. "Hannah needs a hand here with the business. I'm helping where I can, but she needs someone to be at the farm markets. To sell the goods, until Sam's better. Maybe you could..."

Riley shook her head and interrupted. "I'd probably mess that up, too." She turned to face Hannah. "Would you really want a first class screw up like me to help you?"

Hannah hugged her again. "Quit saying that. I think you're special, and I... I like Didi's idea. Would you help us out?"

A glimmer of hopefulness came to Riley's eyes. "Are you serious?"

"Of course."

"I forgot to ask. How's Sam?"

Hannah looked away then brought Riley up to speed.

Riley shook her head. "That poor kid. All the problems he's had, but God always seems to pull him through. The Man above has a purpose for my brother." She took a deep breath. "Maybe this is my purpose. I'll help you out, so you can be with him. Deal?" Riley extended her hand.

Hannah smiled and gripped Riley's hand. "Deal. Like Didi said earlier, we can do anything, if we do it together."

For the first time, Riley smiled.

Didi cleared her throat. "Now, onto more important matters."

The other two women turned to the young blonde. Their words were simultaneous. "What's that?"

Didi's jaw was set. "Setting this thing with Mickey straight. This wasn't your fault *or* your doing. We'll work out a plan to get you two back together."

Riley started to back away. "I don't think that will ever happen."

Didi smiled and reached for her friend's hand. "Oh ye of little faith. Didn't you listen to Hannah? Together, we can do anything."

Riley searched her eyes. "Do you really think there's hope?"

Didi nodded. "Absolutely. We don't always understand it, but God always has a plan." Riley's gaze was on Didi. "Believe in Him, my friend. All you need is faith, and courage to do what He wants."

"I don't know how much of either I've got right now."

Didi winked. "That's why we're here. This is our purpose, to help you. We can do anything, you'll see. And don't forget, we're sisters to the very end."

Chapter 23

E mma kissed Molly's head. "Sweet dreams, little one." The girl had recovered quickly from surgery. Okay, she didn't have a whole lot of stamina, but Emma had never seen a child smile as much as this one did now. *Some of the pain must be gone.* Emma spent the evening cuddling and singing to her new niece.

It was after midnight when she took the elevator to the floor containing the intensive care rooms. *Please God, cure my brother.* Mick's condition had gone downhill rapidly over the last couple of days. His grogginess following surgery had never cleared. They soon discovered why. Her brother had developed pneumonia, and despite antibiotics, it seemed to grow progressively worse.

Emma sat down, assuming the same position in the exact chair she'd occupied for five days in a row. The one where she watched her only brother waste away and writhe restlessly back and forth, murmuring *her* name. Riley. *If that woman was here right now, I'd slap her silly.*

As Emma had every day, she talked to her brother, if for no other reason than to hear noise in the quiet room. "Wake up, Mikey. I need you. And your little girl wants her daddy." She studied the man in the bed. The redness on his forehead, in the area of his stitches was bright red. "Talk to me."

As if in response, his head flopped from side to side. That dreaded word again left his lips. "Riley, Riley, Riley..." His voice trailed off into some unintelligible gibberish.

"Hi, Emma." She turned at the sound of a woman's voice.

"Doc. How's my brother? Any change?"

The doctor didn't respond right away but sat in the chair next to Emma. The woman searched her face. The room was suddenly freezing, forcing Emma to wrap herself in her jacket.

"Mr. Campeau's condition is getting worse. I just got the results of his blood tests and now we understand why. Your brother has sepsis. Do you know anything about this condition?"

"N-no. He's gonna be all right, eh?"

The woman frowned. "I won't lie to you. This is a very bad situation. His condition is critical. Sepsis can be fatal." She pointed to the monitor that displayed his vital signs. "He has a temperature of almost one hundred and five. He's not responding to any of the traditional treatments or medications we've provided. I believe he's in a lot of pain and, as his power of attorney, *you* have a decision to make."

The lady's expression unleashed every fear Emma ever had. *No, God no. Help Mikey please.* Emma turned away to compose herself. She had a hard time comprehending what she'd just heard. "I'm sorry. I don't think I understand."

The physician paused, waiting until Emma again met her eyes. "Mrs. Evans, you need to make a decision, about what's best for him."

Emma swallowed hard. "What decision, doc?"

The other woman's voice was soft. "Yours. This is a very hard choice to make, about what's in your brother's best interest."

Emma sobbed hard. "I, uh, what if, my Mikey... No, no. I can't."

"I can't imagine how hard this must be, but you must decide. You are his power of attorney. We could just give him comfort measures to allow him to pass peacefully, or we can continue to fight by bringing in the crisis intervention team. But you should know, because of his condition, there's a high probability he already has brain damage."

Emma shook her head. "No, let this be a bad dream, please..."

The physician continued. "The man your brother once was..."

Emma placed her hands over her ears. "Don't say it, please?" Emma was losing the battle to maintain her composure.

The other woman paused briefly. "I know this is tough, but I need you to hear this. The man your brother once was may not ever be as you remember him. The intervention team may be able to help, but it's a gamble and could only end up prolonging his pain." The woman studied her. "Mrs. Evans, I need to prepare you for the worst. Your brother's chances of survival aren't good, even with the aid of the intervention team." Emma fought off another sob. "Is there someone you want me to call?"

The strong always protect the weak. Emma shook her head. "No. Please do whatever you can. I don't think I can, I..." She wiped her arm across her face. It was a struggle to get the words out. "I-I n-need him. Please, don't let him die like this. Let's fight this damn thing. That's what he'd want."

The lady nodded. "And you're sure?"

The words were a struggle to emit. "Yes. He's my Mikey."

The doctor stood. "We'll do everything we can. I'll go alert the team. Are you sure there's not anyone I can call for you?"

Emma sat down and then shook her head. "There's no one else."

The doctor turned and ran from the room.

Emma held her brother's hand. "Mikey, you were always there for me. Don't you dare leave me now." The room turned blurry as she fought for control. After a while, a warm touch startled her.

"I'm here for you, and Mickey. You don't have to go through this alone."

Emma looked up at the figure standing behind her.

"Let me help," the woman said.

Emma's arm trembled and her jaw quivered as she stood and faced the person in front of her.

***

Riley combed her hair before climbing under the covers. *So nice of Didi to let me stay here.* Her mind drifted to Mick. While his sister Emma had made it clear she wasn't welcome at the hospital, Riley had kept close tabs on both Mick and Molly. She'd even snuck in several times to hold the little girl. But she didn't have the nerve to face Emma's ire. Didi and Hannah had helped her work out a plan to make things right with Mick, but the timing wasn't perfect, yet.

It took a while, but sleep finally came. After a bit, a vision filled her dreams. She and Mick were walking along a lake, little Molly between them, holding their fingers as the girl ambled along. It was so wonderful, no, *perfect*. Then Molly smiled as she gazed up at Riley. *"Love you, Mommy."* The girl turned to the giant who held her other hand. *"Love you too, Daddy."*

Mick's smile was sad as he let go of the little one's hand. *"And yer Daddy loves you. Always will."* He trained his eyes on Riley. *"Mick's gotta go now, but I'll always be with ya, eh?"*

Are you talking to me or Molly? Riley was confused as she lifted the little girl into her arms. *Where was he going? "Bye, Mick. I'll always love you."* Again, he searched her face, but said nothing. Head down, he turned away.

The voice caught Riley off guard. *"I'll be taking her with me."* She turned to find Emma standing there, arms reaching for Molly.

But the little girl held Riley, tight. *"No, Mommy. I wanna be with you."*

Riley instinctively backed away. *"She can stay with me, until Mick comes back."*

Emma's eyes lacked emotion. *"He isn't coming back, girl. You blew it. It's over, do you understand that? Now hand her to me. She's not yours anymore, she's my responsibility now."* Emma grasped the child and peeled her away from Riley.

"No, no!" Riley again reached for Molly, but Emma shook her head.

"Please, don't cause any more hurt to my family. Just let it be." Emma turned and carried Molly away.

Frantic, Riley turned to Mick. It was surreal. He was standing only a few feet away, but the distance seemed to be miles. His eyes were vacant. *"Mick, help me, please?"* He shook his head, then turned and walked away from her, the image of his body disappearing before her eyes.

Riley fell to the ground and covered her face. *"This can't be happening. Somebody please, please help me!"*

A warm touch on her shoulder took her by surprise. Riley turned and almost fell over when she saw who was standing before her. *Jenna?* Her dead sister was dressed all in white. A comforting glow seemed to surround her. Riley stood and her sister drew her close in an embrace. Jenna's voice was soft. *"It's time, Riley."*

Fear ran rampant in Riley's heart. The recollections of Sam telling her about his encounters with Jenna... after their sister's death... when he was losing his mind after the accident... that Christmas morning when his future with Hannah seemed to be over... in the burning house... they all flooded her mind.

Riley gulped. *"Am I dying? Is my time here over?"*

Jenna smiled and touched Riley's face. Sensations of calmness and serenity flowed from Jenna's hand. *"No, silly. It's time for you to go to your destiny. Your place is at his side. Mickey Campeau is in an awful place right now. He needs to hear your voice... to bring him back from the brink. He's been waiting for you."* Jenna pushed Riley's bangs away from her face. *"Remember what mom and dad taught us? That love can conquer all? Do you remember them telling us that?"* Riley nodded. *"It's time."*

"But... but Emma took Molly away and M-Mick just... vanished. What's that mean?"

Jenna drew her close again. *"That is what* will *be, if you don't act now. Have courage, and follow the plans God has for you."* Jenna released her sister and then began to fade as she backed away. *"Now go, Riley, go. And remember this. I love you. And you'll never walk alone because I'll always be with you, even when you can't see me."*

Riley bolted upright in the bed, soaked in sweat. Her hands were trembling so badly that she dropped her cell when she tried to check the time. The wind whipped against the house, whispering just one word, "Go..."

Throwing off the blankets, Riley pulled on some clothes and ran down the stairs.

***

Riley's heart was in her throat as she stood outside the door to Mick's room. The doctor was talking to Emma while Riley did her best to eavesdrop on the conversation.

Riley's vision blurred as she heard Emma mutter, "There's no one else." Riley stepped to the side as the physician exited the doorway. "Don't you dare leave me now." The words Emma muttered ripped a hole in Riley's heart, but fear also filled her soul. *How will Emma react?* Something strong grew within her chest. *It's now or never. Mickey needs me.* It took everything she had, but Riley stepped into the room.

The voice startled her and it took a few seconds to realize it came from her own throat. "I'm here for you, and Mickey. You don't have to go through this alone."

Emma looked up at her.

"Let me help."

Emma was trembling all over as she advanced toward Riley.

Riley flinched when the woman lunged at her. But instead of hitting her, Emma wrapped her in a tight embrace. "It doesn't look good. I can't face life without my brother. Help him, please? He's been calling for you."

Riley smoothed the hair back from Emma's face. "Everything will be fine. Mickey's going to pull through, wait and see."

Emma eased away, her eyes on Riley's face. "How can you be so sure?"

Riley held the other woman's hands to calm her. "Because you need him. We both... no, all three of us need him. God will see him through." Riley could see the question on Emma's face. "Besides, Jenna told me so."

"Jenna? Who's that?"

Riley touched Emma's shoulders. "Jenna's my sister."

"Thought you only had a brother. Is Jenna some sort of doctor?"

I know this doesn't sound possible. "She's not a doctor. I do have a sister, but she... um... died."

"What? A dead person talked to you?" Emma sniffed Riley's breath. "Have you been drinking?"

Riley shook her head. "No, Emma. Believe me or not, but my sister told me Mickey will make it."

Emma looked at Riley as if she were crazy.

Approaching footsteps caught their attention. The pair moved aside when a medical team burst into the room. The staff placed ice packs under Mick's arms and started another IV. One woman explained what they were doing and spoke to them in words of hope.

As the hours passed, Riley told Emma everything that had happened since Christmas Eve. "I never meant to hurt Mickey. I tried to explain that I was pursuing my dreams. And I didn't know anyone was filming us. Your brother got so mad at me when I handed back the engagement ring. And then he flung it off into the night..." Riley had to pause to control her emotions. "I made a mistake, Emma. I should have talked it over with him, first. I-I only wish I would have listened to my heart. I love your brother. More than anything else." Riley looked away. The expression on Emma's face said it all. *She doesn't believe me.*

Emma's hands were warm where she touched Riley. "There are so many things I don't understand. But one thing I do know. Mikey loves you, too. He's been calling your name for two days." Emma sniffed and looked away. "I'm sorry."

Riley cocked her head. "For what?"

"For yelling at you. Mikey didn't tell me the whole truth about you two, and what happened. Can you forgive me?"

Riley embraced her. "Nothing to forgive."

Emma stood and pushed her chair close to the bed and then pointed to it. "You, you're the key to Mikey getting better. Sit with him and talk to him. Make my brother wake up. I'm gonna go check on Molly a while, eh? Back soon."

After Emma left, Riley sat and held Mick's hand. It was cold as ice. She pressed her lips to his fingers and whispered, "Mickey, I'm here. Where I should have been all along. And I'll be right here when you wake up, forever. I love you." But the man's expression didn't change.

Chapter 24

D idi stumbled out of bed, rushing to try and make it to the commode in time. This was the third day in a row she'd had to throw up when she woke.

It was dark outside, still early on a Saturday morning. Didi made it a point to be extra quiet as she showered and dressed. Didi stopped at Riley's room, cracking the door to check on her friend. *What?* The bed was empty, covers askew. "Riley, are you here?" Silence greeted her. *Maybe she already left for the bakery.*

The thought of food made Didi queasy, but she packed some oatmeal in a bag for later. Despite the early hour, she decided to head to Hannah's. *Wish we would have packed the van last night.* She and Riley had been too exhausted to get ready for the Bird-in-Hand Market.

Didi had just closed the car door when a text message appeared on her phone

I'm at the hospital with Mick. He's got sepsis. Can you cover for me? Please pray for him. Love, Riley

Didi immediately called her friend. Riley answered on the third ring. "Just got your text.

How'd you end up at the hospital? Did Emma call you?"

"No. This will sound strange, but I had a dream... almost a nightmare. Jenna was in it."

Jenna again? Tingles crawled up Didi's neck. "Jenna? Your sister?"

"Yeah. Pretty strange. She told me Mickey needed me and that I should go to him."

What about Mick's sister? "Is... is Emma there?"

"She's down with Molly right now."

"H-how'd she treat you? I know she told you not to see him."

Riley drew a deep breath. "It's okay. We got past it. In fact, she asked me to stay with him. Said she knew I could bring him back. Same thing Jenna said."

"Wow, this is like... unbelievable."

"I know. But Didi, I'm scared. He's not doing well and, I-I'm not sure... Suppose... I just don't know what to do."

Didi struggled for something to say. "Just be with him, Riley. Talk to him. Whisper how much you love him." Curiosity was getting the best of her. "Now tell me more about your dream."

Riley sniffed. "It started out really good. Mickey, Molly and I were taking a walk, but then Emma took Molly away and M-Mickey, he just vanished."

"Oh Riley, I'm sure it was just your fears surfacing in your dream."

"Maybe, but... suddenly Jenna was there, comforting me and..." Didi could hear voices on the other end. "I'll call you back. The medical team's here again. Bye."

"Okay ..." But her friend had disconnected.

The vision of Luke's face was suddenly in front of her. *Please be careful, Luke. I need you.* Thoughts and prayers for both Mick and Luke consumed her mind as she drove to Hannah's Bakery. Lights were already on inside the building when she parked. The smell of baked goods wrapped around her when she opened the door.

Didi entered the kitchen to find Hannah loading up the truck by herself. "Hannah?"

Hannah whipped around, hand over her mouth. "Didi! You scared the daylights out of me. What are you doing here?"

"I got a text from Riley. She asked me to fill in for her today. But I was already on the way."

Hannah's eyebrows furrowed. "Why? Is she sick?"

"No, she's with Mickey."

Disbelief covered Hannah's face. "What?"

Didi told her about the conversation. Hannah sat on a stool and listened. "I don't understand all of this."

"What don't you understand?"

"Jenna. She's gone, but, it's... it's like she's still here. Sam told me she often stays by his side when I'm not there. I'm beginning to wonder if... if they're all crazy. How could Jenna come back from the dead?"

Didi shivered. "I, uh, I don't think Sam and Riley are crazy. A couple of years ago, my dad had a heart attack." She sniffed at the memory. "It seemed like forever until the doctors revived him. And Dad," she stopped to calm herself, "Dad told me what happened while he was gone. Said his parents were there with him. And he talked about the feelings of love that surrounded him. How he could sense what Mom and I were going through. He said love brought him back." Didi wiped her eyes. "I think when you die, you get to take love with you."

Hannah shook her head. "I don't understand this... at all."

Didi nodded. "I think I see what's happening. The love Jenna has for her brother and sister didn't die when she did. I believe she watches over them. Like their guardian angel or something."

The look on Hannah's face signaled her confusion. "So, you believe all this is real?"

"I think so." Didi's stomach suddenly rumbled. *Oh no, gonna throw up.* "Be right back." She made a mad dash to the toilet, barely making it in time. While she was retching, she felt hands lifting her hair back.

"What's wrong? Aren't you feeling well, honey?"

After the wave of nausea passed, Didi stood and wiped her mouth. "I don't know what's come over me. I've been sick for the last three days."

Hannah's eyes grew wide. "All day or just in the morning?"

"A couple hours each morning. Why?"

A smile lit up Hannah's face. "Let me guess. I bet you're late, right?"

What? "Late for what?"

Hannah giggled and pointed at Didi's slim stomach. "You know what I mean. Could it be you're in the expectant mommies club?"

Oh my God! "What? Do you think... no, it couldn't be. We were only together for one night... before Luke left."

Hannah patted her own stomach. "Sometimes, it only takes one try."

"No, Luke's away. How could it... No way... Wait, I'm p-p-pregnant?"

Hannah hugged her. "Maybe, but you better find out. Having a baby changes everything."

Didi's head was spinning. Hannah helped her to the stool. *Luke! What did you do?*

***

"Ma'am? Are you awake?"

Someone was shaking her arm. *Where am I?* Riley glanced around the room. Mick was in a bed with all kinds of medical equipment lining the room. Emma was asleep in the other chair, breathing loudly. A digital clock on the wall read two fifty-five. *Monday morning already?*

"Ma'am? Are you Riley?"

"Yeah." She glanced at the woman shaking her arm. "What's going on?"

"It's Mr. Campeau. He's been calling for you."

Riley glanced at Mick, noticing he was moving, eyes fluttering, lips moving. "Riley, Riley, Riley..."

He's calling my name! Riley was now fully alert. She grabbed his hand. Warmth had returned to his limbs. He was hot all over. "Mickey, it's me. Riley. I'm here."

He struggled to open his eyes. "Where'd ya go? I need ya'. Riley..."

"Baby, I'm right here. At your side."

"Emma, she be takin' Molly. Gotta stop her."

The presence of another hand over hers startled Riley. Emma was also awake now, eyes wide open. "Mikey? I'm here and your little girl is downstairs, waiting on you."

He... he must have been in my dream, too. Mick's eyes appeared to be covered in a hazy fog. "I saw ya take Molly from Riley... Don't... I need her. An' Riley, she just..." His eyes settled on Riley's face. "Riley? Ya came back?"

Riley swallowed hard. "Um-hmm. I'm back. For good."

"But why? I don't understand. Where be Molly?"

Emma answered. "She's downstairs, in her bed."

He squeezed Riley's hand. "An' you? What happened to da angels? They be gone, 'ceptin' you."

Riley realized her hands were shaking. "I don't know, but I'm here, where I should have been all along."

Mick's head relaxed on the bed. "'Kay. Give me a minute. Need a nap. Den, wanna go see her, you an' me, eh? Go see our li'l girl..."

Riley kissed his hand. "Whatever you want." He was out.

Emma touched her shoulder. "Why don't you go get Molly? I'll stay with him in case he wakes." Emma hugged her. "Thank you, Riley. I knew you could bring my brother back to me."

Riley turned to the nurse who was smiling. "Would it be okay to fetch Molly?"

The woman offered her hand. "Yes, yes. Come on, I'll go with you."

It was hard to stand because Riley's knees were shaking so badly. Before she left, she leaned down and kissed Mick's forehead. "We'll be back soon, sweetheart. Both of your girls."

When they arrived at the pediatric floor, the kind lady stopped at the nurse's station while Riley entered the room where Molly lay sleeping. Riley kissed her head and lifted the child in her arms. Suddenly several nurses were there. "She's still got an IV. Let me grab a portable tree and I'll help you."

Molly's sleepy eyes opened. The girl smiled and clung tightly. *Can this be happening? Or is this a dream?*

In less than five minutes, they were at the opening to Mick's room. Emma's eyes were wide as she moved the chairs back so Riley could stand next to the bed. When Molly saw Mick there, she reached for him.

"Not yet, little one." Riley leaned down to whisper in his ear, "Mickey, wake up. Your daughter's here."

Mick took a deep breath and his eyes rolled open. "Riley? Molly?"

Riley gently placed the girl in the crook of his arm.

Mick's eyes closed and he sighed as he gently rested his chin on the baby's head. He reached for Riley, pulling her against him. "Musta died. Dis... dis be heaven." He kissed Riley's cheek. "I love you, Riley Espenshade."

Riley closed her eyes as she held them both. Emma's arms covered all of them. *This surely is Paradise.*

***

Luke combed his hair for a third time before he sat in front of the computer screen. Since being deployed, he'd only been able to speak with Didi twice, but today, he would finally see her face on Skype. He tugged his coat tightly over his frame. *So cold here.* Then Didi's beautiful face filled the screen. *My girl, no, my wife, my everything.* He was speechless.

"Luke, it's so good to see you."

Seeing her again made it hard to breathe. "Oh Deeds, I missed you so much. How are you?"

"Missing you. I love you, Luke Bryan."

He laughed, remembering her pet name for him. "And I love you, Didi... Zinn"

"Got lots of news for you." She turned the phone around. *What the heck?* She was in his house. *No, our house, no... Our home.* But when he left, there hadn't been any furniture. And now? The living room was fully furnished, decorated just as he had described when he told her his dreams the night he first brought her there. "Like it?"

"It's, it's exactly as I imagined it would be. Where'd you get all that stuff?"

She turned the phone around and her image filled the screen. She was obviously walking, heading up the stairs. "When Mom found out, she came in for a week to visit. She and Dad bought all this stuff for us, as a wedding present."

Sadness filled his heart. "I'm sorry we didn't have a big, fancy wedding."

Her lips touched the screen. "I'm not. Just glad you said yes when I asked you to marry me."

"Hey now, I'd have gotten around to it."

Didi giggled. "Beat you to it. When you get back, we'll have a big ceremony, with a gown and cake and flowers. And then something else..."

Wait. *Something else?* What did that mean? "What could possibly be better than marrying you?"

Her face reddened. "You ready for the next surprise?"

There's more? Maybe they bought us a bed. "Yes, please."

Her eyes widened and she smiled. Didi turned the phone around again. The second bedroom upstairs was decorated with Disney characters on the walls. She slowly rotated, showing off the place. A dresser, some kind of table he didn't recognize, then, she turned it to a crib. "Surprise, Daddy."

His breath and pulse both quickened. "What?"

Didi turned the phone to watch him. "You're going to be a daddy, and me a mommy. Luke, I'm pregnant."

The other soldiers in the area looked at him with concerned faces as he cried out, "Deeds! I-I, don't believe it, a daddy? How'd that happen?"

She snickered. "I hope you remember our wedding night. I sure do."

"But it was only... a daddy? When?"

"I'm three months pregnant."

Her image turned blurry before him. "Is it a boy or a girl?"

Her smile was the best thing he'd ever seen. "Doesn't matter. I wanted to wait until you got home. We'll find out together."

"I love you, Deeds. I can't wait…" The sound of an explosion outside reverberated through the room.

One of the platoon leaders screamed, "Mortars. Everyone in the bunkers!"

Didi's face filled with fear. "What's happening?"

A sergeant screamed at him, "Let's go, corporal!"

"Gotta go, Didi. I love you. Everything will be fine."

Didi didn't have a chance to respond before the power went off.

Luke followed the flow of men to the reinforced bunker, hunkering down against the concrete berm. Another mortar shell exploded outside, followed by the roar of American artillery responding to the attack.

Luke closed his eyes and travelled to his happy place to get away from the war. The vision of Didi in her black dress, twirling an umbrella against the backdrop of the Columbia Bridge, that first day. Her face so beautiful, her eyes sparkling. *I'm going to be a daddy. Thank You, God.*

Chapter 25

D idi fussed over Riley's train as her friend stood at the door. As maid of honor, this was Didi's privilege. *But next month, this will be me.* Luke's unit was coming home in three weeks. Her mom, Brenda, already had the wedding plans well in hand.

Emma's voice stole away her thoughts. "Now, this is one beautiful bride." Emma hugged Riley. "I'm sure glad you and Mikey are getting hitched. Always wanted a sister."

Hannah commented, "You do look exquisite, Riley."

Riley smiled and rubbed at her eye.

Didi dabbed it with a hanky. "Stop that, right this instant. Don't ruin your makeup. It took all morning to get it right."

Riley laughed. "Okay, boss." She grabbed Didi tightly. "Thank you."

"For what?"

Riley whispered in her ear, "For taking Jenna's place today. It's like you really are my sister."

Didi's own eyes were now moist. *Means so much to hear you say that.* "I'm honored. I love you, Riley. I just wanted to tell you..."

Riley's dad entered the room and whistled as he took in the bride. "Wow, aren't you the cat's meow? Ready to do this?"

Riley took her father's arm as the wedding march echoed through the loud speakers. The home Mick had built for them in Paradise, less than a mile from the house Luke and Didi would share, was immaculate.

The man turned and surveyed the bridesmaids, but directed his voice at Riley. "You trying to tell Mom and I something?"

Riley looked confused. "What do you mean?"

His face cracked in his smile. He pointed at the women in turn. "Your maid of honor is pregnant, so's Hannah... and Mom told me Emma's pregnant? Does this mean..."

Didi turned to see both Hannah and Emma blush. Hannah was due any day, but Emma had only just found out. Riley hissed at her dad. "Father! I'm not even married yet and you should know I..."

"Everyone hush. It's time to start." The wedding planner handed a basket of flowers to Hannah's daughter, Missi. "Okay, just like we practiced. You go first, honey. Spread the flowers as you stroll, gracefully, ever gracefully."

Missi led the entourage out of the door, dropping rose petals as she walked.

The woman sent the ring bearer to follow, then pointed to Emma. "You're next." Emma gave Riley a final hug.

Hannah also gave Riley a hug. "So happy for you, sis." Hannah departed and Didi stepped in line.

"Didi?" Didi turned to Riley. "Remember, in a couple of weeks, this will be you. And I can't wait to watch you walk down the aisle."

Didi giggled. "You mean waddle?"

"Quit it. Now go."

The wedding planner handed a bouquet to Didi and held the door. Didi stepped into the summer heat. Over three hundred chairs filled the backyard, which had been transformed into one of the Seven Wonders of the World. Tulle, lace and flowers graced almost everything. As Didi followed the procession, her mind drifted. Luke's face filled her thoughts. *Can't wait until you come home, Lucas Bryan, and this is us.*

Before she knew it, she was at her spot at the front of the event. Across the aisle, Mickey Campeau's smile was engaging. So was the expression on Sam Espenshade's face. Sam was the best man. His recovery from the massive burns was still ongoing, but he was finally back at home with Hannah and their daughters.

A reverent silence filled the crowd as Riley strolled down the aisle on her father's arm. When they reached the front, her dad turned, lifting Riley's veil to kiss her.

Mick waited until the older man pulled back, then walked over to hug him. Afterward, Mick dropped to one knee and kissed the hand of his soon-to-be bride before returning to his place beside her.

Didi felt like she was in a dream as she watched the ceremony. Riley's vows were touching, however Mick's made her eyes water, not because of his rough words, but because of the emotion in his voice. "Riley Espenshade. You and me, we be meant to be from the very beginnin'. You see, I was in love wid you way before we met in person. Riley, da first time I saw yer face on the computer, I knowed you were the woman of ma dreams, da one God intended. As if'n da Big Man was shinin' a spotlight on yer picture. And den, when we met at Ashley's weddin', I knowed inside my dreams be finally comin' true."

The big man stopped for a few seconds.

"I tole you many times what my daddy said, 'Da strong, dey take care of da weak'. Usually, I be da strong one. But den, when I was in da hospital... dyin'... that be when I was weak and you be da strong one. Your love brought me back, it be da reason I'm here. And I promise you, Riley, I promise ta love you and cherish ya forever an' a day, an' always put ya first. God declared you an' me to be one, an' who be me not ta listen to da Big Man, eh? Riley Espenshade, you ain't just a pretty face. You gots a purty heart and I be glad to join mine wid yours. Forever."

***

Flight surgeon Comensky tapped Luke's shoulder, yelling to be heard above the noise. "This is going to be a hot LZ, so keep your head low, son. I need you to help me. We've got wounded Marines depending on us."

"Yes, sir." Luke tightened the straps as the airframe rotated into the sky. Both of his brother's Marine Corps units were also deployed in this crazy place. Medics were in such short supply, so Luke volunteered and had been detailed to a medivac unit. This was his twenty-seventh flight mission.

Despite the vibrations and the noise of the helicopter, Luke's mind once again drifted to his bride. *Love you so much, Didi.* The vision of her smile as she stood twirling an umbrella in front of the bridge calmed him as they flew.

The helicopter suddenly bounced hard on the ground. Luke went into automatic mode as he threw off the harness and jumped out of the door. He'd been in hot landing zones twice before, but this one was a nightmare. Marines were deployed helter-skelter along a dry creek bed in a valley. The leathernecks were delivering a steady wall of lead and fire up the hill.

Luke glanced to his left and witnessed heavy fire pouring down onto them from the elevated position. Two American attack choppers rotated into view, firing rockets and delivering a continuous stream of heavy automatic weapon fire to try to suppress the enemy.

Pairs of marines started moving toward the medivac, carrying or dragging the wounded along with them. *Please don't let me look down and find one of my brothers.*

Suddenly the buzz-saw sound of machine guns ceased from the air above them. Luke glanced skyward to see the attack choppers vector off and fly out of sight. One of the Marines started screaming, "Incoming, incoming! Everyone down!"

Luke leapt across the injured man in front of him to cover the soldier's open chest wounds. The ground started to shake. Luke chanced another look at the sky in time to see a blur—a flight of incoming Navy Hornets. The warbirds dropped their ordnance on the hill above him before disappearing from view.

The entire world seemed to split apart. Rocks and debris rained down on all of them, but as everything settled, it was apparent. The fire from the enemy positions above had ceased.

Luke waited until the dust settled before he raised himself off of the wounded man.

Comensky grabbed his arm. "Let's get these boys loaded and get the hell out of Dodge."

The two men directed the loading of the wounded into the chopper, then secured them in litters.

Luke was starting an IV as the chopper lifted off. The flight surgeon shook his arm and pointed at one of the injured. "Triage report, Zinn. Concentrate on these two. The Marines in the front are stable." Comensky was pointing at the man Luke was working on. "I'll see if I can get the bleeding..."

Twenty minutes into the flight, the airship suddenly dipped hard to port, knocking both medics down. The noise and violent light from the explosion almost blinded Luke and momentarily took his hearing. *We've been hit!*

He was trying to hold on when the chopper slammed into the earth. The airframe disintegrated around him and he was ejected down the mountain. Arms up, trying to protect himself, a rock suddenly emerged before Luke's eyes. He bounced off, landing on the ground. Didi's face appeared among the stars and was the last thing he saw before the robed men led him away.

***

The rest of the wedding and reception was a blur. Didi hugged herself over the joy swirling all around her. Mick, Riley and their daughter Molly looked so happy.

Didi was exhausted when it was finally time to leave. *I'll be so glad when Luke gets home.* Thankfully, the wedding planner had a clean-up crew scheduled. Didi said goodbye to everyone and climbed into her car for the short ride home.

When she pulled into the drive, she noticed a black SUV sitting along the curb. Two men got out before she could even exit the car. They both were wearing military dress uniforms.

Didi started to shake uncontrollably as they approached.

The taller of the two men touched a hand to the brim of his hat. "I'm Major Collins and this is Chaplain Darvey. Are you Mrs. Deidre Phillips-Zinn?"

Oh God, no. Please? Didi could only nod.

"It is with regrets that I have to give you this news…"

Chapter 26

Thirty-two months later...

D idi closed her eyes and Luke's face appeared. *I can't wait until you get home.* Didi then unlatched the seatbelt and helped her little man climb out of the vehicle. He was rubbing his eyes. "Did you have a good nap?"

The little boy nodded and reached for her. "Where are we, Mommy?"

Didi picked up her son, brushing his hair with her lips. "We're at the tea house. Aunt Hannah and Aunt Riley are having tea with us. Afterwards, you and I are going shopping. We need to make a present for Daddy." She'd never given up hope her husband was alive. Henry Campbell had often comforted her, reminding her that the military is relentless about searching for—and finding—MIA's. But each day, it seemed to get harder and harder to keep up her faith Luke would return.

The little boy looked into Didi's eyes. "Daddy coming home soon?"

Didi wiped her cheeks. "Someday soon, baby, someday soon." Didi walked through the door.

Sophie Miller greeted the pair and led them to the big table where Riley sat holding her infant son on her lap. The delectable scent of brewed tea wrapped itself around her. Big sister Molly ran to grab Didi's knees. "Aunt Didi!" Didi knelt down and kissed her 'niece'.

"Hi, Molly. I love your dress."

The girl's smile was precious. "Me and Daddy picked it out."

Riley laughed. "You mean 'Daddy and I'."

"Nope. Me and Daddy, not you and Daddy."

Her friend shook her head, then stood for a hug. "How are you, Didi?"

"Surviving. Is Hannah here yet?"

Riley sat down and touched Didi's hand. "She took Jenna to the bathroom." Sam had named his third daughter after their deceased sister.

"What about Angie?" Angie was Hannah's *fourth* daughter.

"She has the sniffles so Mom's taking care of her."

Riley looked so happy. "How about Missi and Beth?"

"Missi? You should know she's at the market with her daddy. Those two are inseparable. And Beth? She's visiting her boyfriend at Temple."

Seems like yesterday when Sam, Riley and I spent Christmas Eve together. Now Beth was dating. "How's Sam taking that?"

Riley shook her head and giggled. "Beth dating a college boy is going over like a lead balloon. But my brother trusts his eldest daughter, no matter what he says. Trusted her enough to let her drive his car to Philly by herself."

"Of course he trusts Beth and she'd die before she let her dad down." Didi turned to find Hannah standing there, smiling as she held little Jenna's hand. Hannah's girl was only four months older than Didi's son.

Didi embraced her friend, holding her tightly for a long while. *My closest friend, like a sister to me.* "How long yet?"

Hannah sat and patted her belly. "Three months, as in ninety days, and about…" Hannah looked up and to the right, "…about two thousand, one hundred and some odd hours, give or take a few."

"And this is the last one?"

Riley giggled and Hannah playfully smacked her sister-in-law's arm. "Let's hope so. The doctor said I'm finally going to give Sam the son he's always wanted."

Didi smiled. "I'm so happy for you."

A server came over and took Didi's order. From the corner of her eye, she saw two women approaching. The one with black hair and the twin dimples was Henry Campbell's wife, Ellie. Didi didn't recognize the other woman, whom Didi suspected was in her early fifties.

"Hey, ladies. Look at this table and all the cute kids. Everyone, this is my Aunt Katie. She and Uncle Jeremy are in town for a romantic getaway." Ellie introduced Riley and Hannah before turning to Didi. "And this is my friend Didi Zinn and her son Lucas."

Didi noticed the change in Katie's expression. *She's heard.* The sadness in the older woman's hazel eyes betrayed her smile. "Nice to meet you, Didi."

She extended a hand to the little boy sitting on Didi's lap. "It's a pleasure to meet you, Lucas."

Didi gave her a genuine smile. "We call him LBJ."

Katie's eyes raised in a question mark. "LBJ?"

Didi nodded. "After his father, Lucas Bryan, Junior."

The older woman wiped her cheek. "I'm sorry, Didi. Ellie told me about your husband. Jeremy was in the Rangers before we married. I can't imagine..."

Didi held a hand in front of her. *She means no harm.* "It's fine, but I don't want to go there."

Katie's face reddened. "I didn't mean to... Forgive me." The woman straightened up. "It was such a pleasure to have met you all." She reached for Didi's hand and squeezed it. "You're a hero. Just like your husband. Goodbye." The two women walked away.

Hannah pulled Didi against her. "I've met Katie before. She's as nice as can be, heart of gold. She meant no offense."

"I know. They never do. But then they get that look in their eyes, like, 'oh, so *you're* the one'. The one whose husband didn't make it home." Didi shook her head. "I was interviewing this woman the other day. As we were chatting before the interview, she asked if I knew the reporter who'd lost her husband in the war. And she told me all about the advice she wanted to give her. 'She should just move on. Too young to be an old maid. A woman her age has needs.' It's so easy to judge when you aren't the one standing in my shoes."

Glancing across the table, both Hannah and Riley were watching her with keen interest. It was Riley who asked, "What did you say to her?"

Didi waited until after the server delivered her pot of tea before continuing. "I told her it was me. Said I didn't care what she thought." Didi stopped to keep from sobbing. "I told the busybody that our love was eternal. There will never be another man for me, ever. Because when I married Luke, I married for life."

Riley's eyes were glistening. "I am so proud of you. It takes so much courage to do what you do."

Didi sipped her tea. *Needs more sugar.* She dropped two more cubes of brown sugar in the cup. "This week, his mom told me I should move on. Same words his dad said last year. 'We understand if you want to re-marry.' I'm sorry, but they don't get how much that hurts." Hannah was dabbing her eyes now. "Luke's memory is with me everywhere I go. I feel his touch, hear his voice. He's alive, I tell you. If nowhere else in this universe, Lucas Donald Zinn lives in my heart, and will be with me until I draw my last breath."

"Mommy, I gotta go potty." LBJ was pulling at her arm.

"Sure, sweetie. Mommy will take you."

Didi stood, staring at the women across the table. They both had watery eyes. "When we get back, I'll need your help."

Riley nodded. "Anything you need. Say the word and it's yours."

"Good. LBJ and I need an idea for a craft to make for his daddy. Maybe you can find something on Pinterest. Luke's birthday is coming up, you know?"

***

It was freezing in the hut. The wind howled, shaking the lean-to. Luke's mouth was so dry, he couldn't even pull his lips apart. His mind drifted back to that horrible night. When he and Comensky were captured and chained together. For days, they'd been bound and blindfolded until they arrived here, wherever in the hell *here* was. And the miserable iron band on his leg had been attached to him since that first night. Wherever the surgeon went, Luke had to follow.

One of their captors spoke enough English to communicate. The chieftain's son had been sick. And as long as they kept him alive, they would live, too. Cure the boy, and they'd be released. But if the child perished, they'd pay with their lives, slowly and painfully.

Something crawled across his legs. *The rats are back.* Luke lacked the energy to even open his eyes anymore. The little boy had suffered from Type I Diabetes. And the two Americans had done everything they possibly could. But when the black market source of insulin disappeared, the kid slowly wasted away. The poor child passed ten days ago. Luke wasn't surprised by the beating he and Cameron Comensky had received, but was puzzled when his captors didn't execute them. Instead, they locked them in this shed... and seemed to forget them. Luke and the doctor finally realized they were being starved to death. Cameron had quit moving the day before. Luke was pretty sure his friend was dead. Now Luke held a vigil, waiting to join his buddy.

He may not have the physical energy to move anymore, but his mind was still sound. He travelled through space and time. To the day he'd met her. *Love you so much, Deeds.* Everything about that first day filled his soul. Her smile, her voice. That precious laughter. The tingle from the touch of her hand against his skin. The subtle scent of plumeria from Didi's perfume. The way his heart warmed as they spoke. *You took me to Paradise that day, Deeds.* How he'd laughed when she misunderstood their first assignment. *You thought I was going to take you home to meet my folks.*

An annoying throbbing noise interrupted his thoughts. He willed himself to return to his Didi's memories and finally forced the din from his mind. He remembered how his world seemed to end when she fell off the steps at Bushkill. And how he'd jumped over the railing, intent on saving her life... or joining her in death. *But now, I'm going first, Deeds, to a place where you can't follow. Please always remember how much I love you.*

Then he wondered about his child. *Did we have a boy or a girl?* He'd never know. Maybe God would tell him, if they allowed soldiers into Heaven.

Rodent feet pitter-pattered across his chest, making him shiver. The wind was picking up, making the walls rattle. And what was that incessant roar? He'd heard that sound before in his life, but Luke's fuzzy mind couldn't connect the dots. Until... bursts of weapon fire seemed to be right outside the shack. Dust settled from the rafters when multiple explosions shook the earth. The concussions were drowning out the wind. *Choppers?*

An increasing firefight seemed to be raging right outside his door, but Luke no longer cared. *No more war for me.* The world was growing dim. Didi's smile lit his mind, his wife's face his only care. Warmth and happiness filled and surrounded him. *This is it, Deeds. You and me, forever.*

The darkness retreated and light shone brightly from above, then all around him. A familiar voice he couldn't quite identify kept repeating, "I'm so proud of you. So proud you're my son, Luke."

Didi's scent filled his soul, the taste of her kisses consumed him. Luke gave in. *I'm ready, Father. Take me home, please, take me to paradise.*

***

LBJ was settled in for his nap. Didi watched the child for a few moments. Her son's little eyes twitched as he dreamed, the same way Luke's had. *No, like they still do.* She kissed her little man and trotted down the stairs. The nagging voices and feelings of despair were rapidly overwhelming her again. *Mom said to call when this happened.* In the early days, the debilitating feelings occurred almost daily. She needed her mom so often that her parents sold their business, retired and moved to Pennsylvania. They now lived in Gap. Far enough away that they wouldn't be a bother, but close enough to show up at a moment's notice when needed.

Luke, why'd you have to volunteer for that stupid mission? Why did her man have to be a hero? The panic attack was well underway. It was a struggle, but she managed to extract the cell phone from her purse. Didi's hands were shaking so badly that it took four tries before she hit the correct speed dial for her mother.

"Hey, Didi. How's my baby?"

It was a struggle just to speak. "Mom. This, this... it's is a really bad day. I n-n-need you. You have time to come over?"

"Of course. What's wrong, honey?"

Before Didi could answer, there was a knock on the door. "H-h-hold on a second. There's someone on the porch." Didi pulled the door open. She recognized the two men dressed in military attire. "What? God, please, no..." The cell fell to the floor and she covered her ears to get away from the horrible noise. The sound of her own screams.

Epilogue

Luke hobbled to the rear of the aircraft, taking a center seat. *Finally going home.* But what would he discover when he got there? His first thought after rescue was to call Didi. But then Cameron told him about the call to his own wife. *How did that man survive? I thought he was dead.* But his friend had made it. They shared a hospital room in Germany. Cameron's face was before him as the man hung up the phone.

"Did you talk to her?"

His friend wiped his cheeks. "Yeah."

"Bet she was surprised."

The man grunted. "Sure was. Wish I hadn't called."

A chill climbed across Luke's shoulders. "Why? What did she say?"

The good doctor took a ragged breath. "Thought I was dead. Terry remarried. She's expecting."

The stewardess touched his arm, handing him a glass of champagne. "From the pilot, in honor of your homecoming."

"Thanks." Luke stared at the glass for a long time before sipping it. Did Deeds move on, too? He returned the glass and fell into a deep and uneasy sleep. Probably thought I was dead. Why would she wait? Visions of Didi, holding his child, yet wearing another man's ring tortured him worse than his captors ever had. Maybe I'll head out west when I get there and forget about returning to Paradise. It would be better not to know than to see his wife with another man.

The vibrations of the wheels locking into place interrupted his nightmare. Reaching for the seatback in front of him, he braced for the landing. The voice of the stewardess was just background noise as she relayed gate numbers for connecting flights. The sound of the engines winding down seemed like the end of his life. Some life, huh? Coming home to find everything I wanted is gone.

A man's voice came across the speakers. "Ladies and gentlemen, this is the Captain speaking. I ask that you remain in your seats for just a moment. Flight 187 is proud to have on board a real American hero, Luke Zinn. Corporal Zinn is making his way home after 967 days in captivity. Welcome home, son. You're a hero in our eyes."

Luke unlatched his belt, every eye focused on him. He struggled to his feet. A man across the aisle helped retrieve his duffle from the overhead bin. Clapping started, first in his section, then all along the aircraft. Every passenger stood, cheering for him. Luke's eyes were blurry as he used two canes to walk down the aisle. The pilot and co-pilot were standing outside the cockpit and took turns shaking his hand.

Finally, he was in the jetway. Music greeted him. The Star Spangled Banner? He emerged through a door to rousing cheers from everyone in the airport.

He gazed over the crowd, until his eyes locked on a familiar face. She was wearing the same dress she'd worn that first day. He couldn't help it. Luke lost his composure as he dropped both canes and threw his arms wide open.

***

Didi was a bundle of nerves. Since the moment those two officers told her Luke had been rescued, she longed to hear his voice. She tried to contact him, but they told her he wasn't ready to talk to her yet. *Why?*

Not knowing what condition Luke would be in when he deplaned, she'd travelled alone to greet her husband. So LBJ remained home, with her parents. *At least I'm not entirely alone.* His unit had arranged for a limo to take her to the airport.

Her own television station had obtained permission from TSA so Didi could be waiting at the gate when Luke got off the plane. When she arrived at the airport, it was no surprise the media was there, as was a military band.

His plane finally taxied to the gate. *Please help me stop shaking.* And then a voice came over the intercom, asking everyone to stand as a former POW stepped foot on his native land again.

Her cheeks were wet when the band started playing the National Anthem. And then, Didi's heart caught in her throat. There he was, using two canes to steady himself when he walked through the door. His face scanned the crowd. *I'm right here, Luke. Waiting.*

Luke's eyes finally landed on her. He dropped the canes and opened his arms, getting out one word before he lost it. "Deeds?"

Didi ran, grabbing hold of her husband as if her life depended on him. As tightly as he'd held her at Bushkill Falls when he'd saved her life. Flashes of bright light were all around them, but neither cared. Their lips blended together and for the first time in over forty months, the world was right.

***

Didi didn't have a clue how they made it past the crowds to the limo. Words weren't needed as they held each other tightly. It was a good twenty minutes before he spoke. "I was afraid... so afraid you wouldn't be here... waiting on me."

She dried his tears. "Of course I'd be here, silly. I'm your wife and I've been waiting for you, every single second of every day."

"How is everyone?"

Didi sniffed. *This is going to be hard.* "Your mom's doing well, as is the rest of your family. But I've got bad news." She faltered and looked away.

Luke lifted her head. "It's my dad, isn't it?"

She wiped her cheeks. "He died last fall. Lung cancer. Dad was such a great man. The media was a circus outside our house when they found out you were missing, until your dad came and sent them packing. The day they told us you were missing, he took down his Marine Corps flag and raised the POW-MIA flag. And he lowered the American flag to half-staff. Swore he'd keep it there until you returned home. He loved me like I was his daughter.

On his deathbed, he made me promise that when you returned, that... that he wanted you to know how proud he was. He wanted you, his hero, to raise Old Glory back up, and... and to know how much he loved you."

Luke studied her face. "The day they rescued us, I heard Dad's voice. Told me how proud he was of me. I believe he was there with me. Kind of crazy, huh?"

She couldn't help herself. Didi kissed his lips, soft and long. "No. I really believe there's a spiritual world we can't see all around us." His mouth fell open when she told him about how Jenna saved Sam and how the dead woman encouraged Riley to go to Mick as well. "Mickey almost died, but Riley's love brought him back. They're married now, and do you remember that little girl, Molly?" Luke nodded. "They adopted her. And they just had a son, too."

He squeezed her hands tightly. "You haven't m-mentioned o-o-our ch-child. I-is everything okay with him, or is it a her?"

Warmth ran up her arms. "I'm sorry, I forgot to tell you, Daddy. You have a son. I named him after you, Lucas Bryan."

His eyes welled. "A son? We have a little boy?"

"Um-hmm. He looks just like you."

"And you named him Lucas Bryan Zinn?"

"Yep, but I call him LBJ – Lucas Bryan Junior." She grabbed out her phone and pulled up a recent picture.

Luke ran his sleeve over his face. "A son. I'm sorry I wasn't there. He won't even know me."

Didi laughed. "Oh yes, he will."

"How could he even know what I look like?"

I love you so much. "Because I've shown him your photo each and every day. Told him all about you. He keeps asking when Daddy's coming home."

Luke touched her hair. "You're incredible. Even though I wasn't here, you kept my memory alive. Suppose I didn't make it?"

She held him tightly. "I knew you were alive. I felt you in my heart."

The divider between the driver and the rear slid down. A man's voice addressed them. "Excuse me, but you might want to see this. We're getting off the Pennsylvania Turnpike here, at Denver. Just watch." The limo curved around the off-ramp. As soon as the vehicle passed through the toll booth, they were waiting—four State Police vehicles turned on their lights. Two pulled in front of them and two dropped in line behind them.

Luke looked at Didi. "What's going on?"

Didi shrugged.

The driver laughed. "I'm sure you remember how bad the traffic is on Route 222 and US 30. The troopers are here to clear your way home." A few minutes later, he again addressed them. "Check out this sign." He pointed to a marker which read: The Lucas Donald Zinn Highway. "The state renamed this section of highway after you, Corporal Zinn. Keep your eyes straight ahead." The car was descending down a long hill toward US 322 at Ephrata.

Didi's heart was in her throat when she caught sight of the display. Two fire trucks extended their ladders across the highway. A large American flag was strung between them, along with a banner that said, "Welcome home, Luke." People were along the road, waving.

Didi glanced across the seat at her husband. His chin was quivering. The closer they got to Lancaster, the more people were gathered along the road, on overpasses, along the berm. Hundreds of people waved flags and held up signs, welcoming her husband home. The entourage passed through Lancaster, getting off at the Old Philadelphia Pike. The sides of Pennsylvania Route 340 were crowded, thousands of people now waving and cheering.

The convoy finally pulled into their drive. Everyone Luke really cared about was waiting outside their home, except his father. It was hard to keep the tears inside. *I've waited forty long months for this.* Didi turned his head toward her. His cheeks were also wet. "Welcome home, Luke. I love you so much."

"Love you, too, Deeds."

The car door flew open and his mother, Angel, reached for him. Didi stayed close, watching as person after person greeted and hugged her husband. The sun was setting when the last of the crowd finally left. Luke turned to his wife. "Is our son here? I want to meet, and hold my boy."

Didi nodded and led him into the house. Her parents were there patiently waiting inside. Brenda walked over and kissed her son-in-law. Phil hugged him, pounding his back. They said goodbye and closed the door behind them.

"Come with me. LBJ's in the next room watching a video." Didi took his hand and led her husband into the room.

The little boy came running to Didi. "Mommy."

Didi's eyes were blurry as she turned the child toward Luke. "LBJ, meet your..."

The boy's eyes grew large and he reached for Luke. "Daddy!"

Luke held his son, kissing him for the first time.

Her husband was too choked up to speak. Didi wrapped her arms around both of them. "Welcome home, Daddy."

He found her lips. "Thank you, Deeds."

Didi touched his face. "It was just a house, until you walked in. Now it's a home."

He kissed her hand. "Not just a home. This... this is Paradise."

The End

Get exclusive

never-before-published content!

www.chaswilliamson.com

A Paradise Short Story

Download your free copy of
Skating in Paradise today!

Other Books by this Author

Seeking Forever (Book 1)

Kaitlin Jenkins long ago gave up the notion of ever finding true love, let alone a soulmate. Jeremy is trying to get his life back on track after a bitter divorce and an earlier than planned departure from the military. They have nothing in common, except their distrust of the opposite sex.

An unexpected turn of events sends these two strangers together on a cross-country journey—a trip fraught with loneliness and unexpected danger. And on this strange voyage, they're forced to rely on each other—if they want to survive. But after the past, is it even possible to trust anyone again?

Seeking Forever is the first book of Chas Williamson's Seeking series, the saga of the Jenkins family over three generations.

Will Kaitlin and Jeremy ever be the same after this treacherous journey?

Seeking Happiness (Book 2)

Kelly was floored when her husband of ten years announced he was leaving her for another woman. But she isn't ready to be an old maid. And she soon discovers there's no shortage of men waiting in line.

Every man has his flaws, but sometimes the most glaring ones are well hidden. And now and then, those faults can force other people to the very edge, to become everything they're not. And when that happens to her, there's only one thing that can save Kelly.

Seeking Happiness is the second book of Chas Williamson's Seeking series, the saga of the Jenkins family over three generations.

Ride along with Kelly on one of the wildest adventures you can imagine.

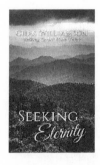

Seeking Eternity (Book 3)

At eighteen, Nora Thomas fell in love with her soulmate and best friend, Stan Jenkins. But Nora was already engaged to a wonderful man, so reluctantly, Nora told Stan they could only be friends. Stan completely disappeared (well, almost), from her world, from her life, from everywhere but Nora's broken heart.

Ten painful years later, the widow and mother of two was waiting tables when she looked up and found Stan sitting in her section. But she was wearing an engagement ring and Stan, a wedding ring. Can a woman survive when her heart is ripped out a second time?

Seeking Eternity is the third book of Chas Williamson's Seeking series, a glimpse at the beginning of the Jenkins' family saga through three generations.

Will Nora overcome all odds to find eternal happiness?

Seeking the Pearl (Book 4)

Eleanor Lucia has lived a sad and somber life, until she travels to London to open a hotel for her Aunt Kaitlin. For that's where Ellie meets Scotsman Henry Campbell and finally discovers true happiness. All that changes when Ellie disappears without a trace and everyone believes she is dead, well almost everyone.

But Henry and Ellie have a special bond, one that defies explanation. As if she were whispering in his ear, Henry can sense Eleanor begging him to save her. And Henry vows he will search for her, he will find her and he will rescue her, or spend his last breath trying.

Seeking the Pearl is the exciting finale of Chas Williamson's Seeking series, the culmination of the three generation Jenkins' family saga.

Henry frantically races against time to rescue Ellie, but will he be too late?

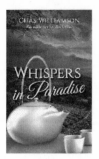

Whispers in Paradise (Book 1)

Ashley Campbell never expected to find love, not after what cancer has done to her body. Until Harry Campbell courts her in a fairy tale romance that exceeds even her wildest dreams. But all that changes in an instant when Harry's youngest brother steals a kiss, and Harry walks in on it.

Just when all her hopes and dreams are within reach, Ashley's world crumbles. Life is too painful to remain in Paradise because Harry's memory taunts her constantly. Yet for a woman who has beaten the odds, defeating cancer not once, but twice, can anything stand in the way of her dreams?

Whispers in Paradise is the first book in Chas Williamson's Paradise series, stories based loosely around the loves and lives of the patrons of Sophie Miller's Essence of Tuscany Tea Room.

Which brother will Ashley choose?

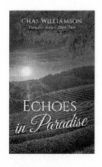

Echoes in Paradise (Book 2)

Hannah Rutledge rips her daughters from their Oklahoma home in the middle of the night to escape a predator from her youth. After months of secrecy and frequent moves to hide her trail, she settles in Paradise and ends up working with Sam Espenshade, twelve years her junior. Sam wins her daughters' hearts, and earns her friendship, but because of her past, can she ever totally trust anyone again?

Yet, for the first time since the death of her husband, Hannah's life is starting to feel normal, and happy, very happy. But a violent attack leaves Sam physically scarred and drives a deep wedge between them. To help heal the wounds, Hannah is forced from her comfort zone and possibly exposes the trail she's tried so hard to cover.

Echoes in Paradise is the second book in Chas Williamson's Paradise series, an exciting love story with Sophie Miller's Essence of Tuscany Tea Room in background.

When the villain's brother shows up on Hannah's doorstep at midnight on Christmas Eve, were the efforts since she left Oklahoma in vain?

Courage in Paradise (Book 3)
Sportscaster Riley Espenshade returns to southcentral Pennsylvania so she can be close to her family while growing her career. One thing Riley didn't anticipate was falling for hockey's greatest superstar, Mickey Campeau, a rough and tall Canadian who always gets what he wants... and that happens to be Riley. Total bliss seems to be at her fingertips, until she discovers Mickey also loves another girl.

The 'other girl' happens to be Molly, a two-year old orphan suffering from a very rare childhood cancer. Meanwhile, Riley's shining career is rising to its zenith when a new sports network interviews her to be the lead anchor. Just when her dream job falls into her lap, Mickey springs his plan on her, a quick marriage, adopting Molly and setting up house.

Courage in Paradise is Chas Williamson's third book in the Paradise series, chronicling the loves and lives of those who frequent Sophie Miller's Essence of Tuscany Tea Room.

Riley is forced to make a decision, but which one will she choose?

Stranded in Paradise (Book 4)

When Aubrey Stettinger is attacked on a train, a tall, handsome stranger comes to her assistance, but disappears just as quickly. Four months later, Aubrey finds herself recuperating in Paradise at the home of a friend of a friend.

When she realizes the host's brother is the hero from the train, she suspects their reunion is more than a coincidence. Slowly, and for the first time in her life, Aubrey begins to trust—in family, in God and in a man. But just when she's ready to let her guard down, life once again reminds her she can't trust anyone. Caught between two worlds, Aubrey must choose between chasing her fleeting dreams and carving out a new life in this strange place.

Stranded in Paradise is the fourth book in the Paradise series, chronicling the loves and lives of those who frequent Sophie Miller's Essence of Tuscany Tea Room.

Will Aubrey remain *Stranded in Paradise*?

Christmas in Paradise (Book 5)
True love never dies, except when it abandons you at the altar.

Rachel Domitar has found the man of her dreams. The church is filled with friends and family, her hair and dress are perfect, and the honeymoon beckons, but one knock at the door is about to change everything.

Leslie Lapp's life is idyllic – she owns her own business and home, and has many friends – but no one special to share her life... until one dark and stormy afternoon when she's forced off the highway. Will the knock at her door be life changing as well?

When love comes knocking at Christmas, will they have the courage to open the door to paradise?

About the Author

Chas Williamson's lifelong dream was to write. He started writing his first book at age eight, but quit after two paragraphs. Yet some dreams never fade...

It's said one should write what one knows best. That left two choices—the world of environmental health and safety... or romance. Chas and his bride have built a fairytale life of love. At her encouragement, he began writing romance. The characters you'll meet in his books are very real to him, and he hopes they'll become just as real to you.

True Love Lasts Forever!

Follow Chas on
www.bookbub.com/authors/chas-williamson

Enjoyed this book?
Please consider placing a review on Amazon!

Made in the USA
Middletown, DE
16 September 2021